JB SCHROEDER

faking it together

Love That Lasts

BOOK 1

Two Feet
Press

11923 NE Sumner St., Ste 843916
Portland, Oregon 97220

Print Edition 1.0
ISBN-13: 978-1-943561-19-3

❀ Created with Vellum

To Kate
whose support, brainstorming prowess, and
infectious laughter were essential
to the creation of this series

1

———

Jake Walker stood in swim trunks, bare feet, and goosebumps on an outcrop of rock and contemplated the thirty-foot jump while ignoring the jeers and ribbing from the other pasty-white New York City traders across the water. This spot of the creek was the highest outcrop a person could scramble up to through the trees and growth without breaking his neck, at least according to the local guide from True Springs, Pennsylvania, where they'd come for a team-building event.

Team building, my ass, Jake thought. This was just another way for these yahoos to compete.

The water below was crisp, cold and—judging from his previous jump on the lower rock shelf—deep enough that he'd survive.

He leaned over to get a better look, and nerves skittered across his chest. He wasn't afraid of heights, but this was really high. And it wasn't even part of the Delaware River. This was just some creek or stream that fed into it.

But more than anything, if he got injured or died, he didn't want it to be among this miserable crew.

Somebody hollered, "Come on, Walker, just *walk* right off."

Lame. They'd direct their attention to somebody else the second he surfaced.

Nothing for it. He swam with these sharks daily. Didn't matter they actually had some water today.

One, two…screw it.

Jake leapt, adrenaline surging, and grabbed his nose just before he went under. Down, down, and then a second of buoyancy before he started pulling up with his arms. He popped out of the water and shook his head hard to clear some water. He even whooped—'cause yeah, it'd been a rush.

He had just crested the slippery ridge peppered with rocks and tree roots, when he saw Reese Statler—who'd already jumped but was clearly afraid of heights—get shoved straight over the edge by one of the senior traders. Dirtbag. That move was dangerously stupid. Because if Reese didn't clear the ledges below…

Jake scrambled to the edge and peered over. He waited…and waited.

Finally, he heaved a sigh of extreme relief when Reese came up bright red and cursing. The epithets bounced off the cliff walls.

Jake echoed the sentiment.

———

By the next morning—despite a killer breakfast at a little place called the Heartland that reminded him of his family's diner in Pittsburgh's Strip District—Jake couldn't wait to leave True Springs.

Under different circumstances, he'd get a kick out of this charming little Pennsylvania town. On the eastern edge of the Poconos and very near the New York border, it was only an hour and a half from New York City. And the surrounding countryside, all hills and leafy green and curving two-lane roads, reminded him of the suburbs of Pittsburgh—and made him long for home.

He'd had enough of his coworkers, though. Bad enough to spend the week with them. Torture to waste a weekend in the same company. Especially when he'd been trying to figure a way out of this company, maybe this career, for nearly a year now.

The senior traders and execs had taken off one by one as their town cars arrived to take them home to their 2.4 kids in Darien and Ridgefield and wherever else. The rest of the young schmucks like him sat in the cozy lobby area of the Sweetwater Inn, a boutique hotel and the only place to stay right in town. While they waited for a private bus to cart them back to the city, every single trader had his head bent to a laptop or cell phone.

Rather than sit with them, Jake hovered near the door. He grabbed a brochure off the front desk.

True Springs, according to the pamphlet, catered to tourists—especially those looking for a little romance in their lives. Apparently, legend had it that the spring water held lovers' magic ever since a couple—Miles and Adele Hoffman—reunited after World War II. At the very moment they kissed, the bus ticket that brought them back together just happened to float into the town fountain.

Ah, Jake thought, that explained the grand fountain in

the center of town. It sported a life-sized statue of a couple in a lip lock in forties-era clothing *and* a spigot. Not to mention that everything in this town spelled l-o-v-e love. There was a Lover's Lane, Valentine's Cafe, Sweet-on-You Shoppe, and who knew what else.

That also maybe explained why Carly, the executive admin who'd coordinated this trip, chose the destination. Because honestly, it was an odd place to take a bunch of traders from the city. He'd suspected Carly had a thing for Reese. Jake glanced around but didn't spot either of them. Huh.

The manager of the Sweetwater Inn, Maddie Kate, appeared next to him.

"Feel free to take that," she said with a grin. "You might want to come back sometime soon. Maybe with somebody?"

Jake reared back a bit. Awfully pushy, wasn't she?

"I'm not looking to romance anybody at the moment," Jake said. He was taking a breather from girlfriends. The last one—who preferred clubbing until all hours over dinner or a show or nearly anything—couldn't stand his early trading hours and only lasted a couple of months. He couldn't even remember what attracted him to her in the first place.

She shrugged. "You drank the water here, didn't you?"

"I didn't exactly take a cup over to the spigot." Jake hooked his thumb in the direction of the fountain.

Maddie Kate chuckled and pushed a chunk of blond curls away from her face. "Doesn't matter. Practically every chef and bartender and baker in this town mixes a few drops into everything they make. And really, if you even brushed your teeth—"

"I definitely brushed my teeth," he said.

"Well then," she said, flipping her palms up, "you'll find your true love whether you come back or not."

"Don't tell me you buy into all this?" He waved the brochure.

She smiled again. "I know it sounds crazy, but I've seen it in action too many times. I no longer doubt."

A vision of laughing brown eyes and a cloud of the softest dark hair flashed through Jake's mind, right along with the scent of cinnamon.

Sadie Evans.

The girl that had featured in almost all of his teenage fantasies—although he had always been careful to treat her no differently than one of his brothers. Most of the time, anyway. There'd been that *one* kiss—that single but all-consuming kiss that had screwed with his foundation and turned him into some kind of Leaning Tower of Pisa. Still standing, but never quite the same.

He shook his head—why had he thought of her today? Breathing in all this greenery and then inhaling that diner breakfast must really have brought him back in time. Sadie had worked—still did, actually—at his parents' diner, The Wanderlust, along with him and his brothers.

He spotted the small luxury bus out the front window, so he stuffed the brochure back into its holder and told Maddie Kate, "It's a great hotel. Thanks."

He didn't think he'd be back. Certainly not anytime soon. He needed to figure out his life before he dragged a woman into it.

He grabbed his duffel bag and slipped out the door.

He'd already known he halfway despised his work—

and, therefore, pretty much his life—but this event had made it crystal clear.

The guys he worked with were nearly all arrogant, self-important, and brash. Maybe that was a vast generalization, but in his company it seemed to hold true. And no matter the caliber of people, trading was a high-octane, stress-filled, empty career.

Did he make good money? Yeah. *Really* good money. He traded options. When he'd tried to explain it to his parents, his dad had scratched his head and said, "Okay, so basically you sell air."

Uh… No. But he totally got that there was something horribly intangible about it. Experience, knowledge, instinct, and especially accuracy actually mattered—but it was still like placing bets. All day long, every day. At this point he didn't feel especially good about that. The thrill had worn off. He was tired of it all.

But where did he go from here? What options—ha ha—were out there for a twenty-eight-year-old trader who was already washed up inside? Would he commit career suicide if he left? Did he care? And what else would he even do?

As he greeted the driver and stepped onto the bus, his phone rang. It was his mom. He would have liked to talk to her but didn't care to with his coworkers listening. He let it go to voicemail, figuring he could call his parents once he was back in his apartment.

Except a notification for voicemail didn't show up. By the time he'd slid into a seat, a text from his mom did. It said: *Call me right away. IMPORTANT.*

Jake frowned and called her back.

"Mom?"

"Jake," she said.

Just that one word, his name breathed out, and he heard it all: relief, dread, shock, grief.

And he knew that something was very, very wrong.

———

The next morning, the receptionist of Hillendorf's Funeral Home led Jake down a short, carpeted hallway, knocked on the heavy door, then pushed it open without waiting for an answer. They'd been expecting him for a while now, but his flight into Pittsburgh had been delayed at landing. The small group clustered inside all stood: his mom, Rita; his brothers, Jeremy and Jonah; and the director, Hap Hillendorf.

Rita threw her arms wide, and Jake stepped into them.

"Mom," he said, squeezing her hard. "I'm so sorry it took me so long." He'd hoped to be here last night but couldn't get a same-day flight. And he'd considered renting a car, but Rita was adamant that he not drive while upset.

She pulled back to look up at him, still holding his arms. Tears swam in her eyes, and although she was made up, he could see that she must have used plenty of tissues.

"Please," she said. "I'm just so glad you're here now." She patted his arm and stepped aside.

Jake embraced Jeremy, the eldest Walker brother, first. He was in his usual black jeans but had capitulated to wearing a black button-down shirt rather than the band t-shirts he generally preferred. His expression was nearly always serious, but Jake could see the strain around his eyes today. They didn't speak, just shared a look, lips pressed into hard lines.

Jonah, the youngest, was next. More hugging and back pounding. Jonah was fighting crying, and only managed, "Sucks, huh?"

"It sure as hell does," Jake said tightly. What did you say at a time like this? There was so *much* that should be said, and yet nothing seemed adequate.

Jake reached to shake the funeral director's hand. "Hap," he said.

A short, trim, middle-aged man with a full head of white hair, Hap always wore a pleasant, serene expression. He'd helped the Walkers bury all of Jake's grandparents, too. A first-name basis seemed appropriate, although Jake always thought the name an ironic one, given the Hillendorfs' business. Still, when a guy was born Harold the third, the family had no choice but to shorten it to something.

"Jake," Hap said, squeezing his hand. "I'm so sorry about your dad. Chuck was the best kind of man. He will be sorely missed."

"Thank you." The swelling in Jake's throat prohibited him from saying more.

"Take some time together as a family," Hap said, making eye contact with Rita before he slipped out the door. The man was truly a master at managing people's comfort during difficult times.

Jake let out a breath.

"Come sit," Rita told him. "We've already covered most of the details. We were just talking about who should be pallbearers."

Jake swallowed, still trying to dislodge the lump in his throat.

"Us three, of course," Jeremy said.

"And Uncle Mark," Jonah said. That was his mom's sister Reenie's husband.

"So we need two more?" Jake said.

Jeremy suggested cousins. Jonah suggested other uncles. Rita wondered about her husband's best friends.

Jake had a better idea—one that made his nose tingle and his eyes burn from trying not to cry. "It should be Sadie," he said. Chuck and Rita had become surrogate parents to her, and numerous times over the last twenty-four hours, he'd wondered how she was holding up. This would hit her hard.

"Traditionally it's men, but Sadie's strong," Jonah said, while Jeremy nodded.

Rita burst out in tears.

"It's okay, Mom," Jake said, and leaned in to squeeze her knee.

She grabbed a wad of tissues off Hap's desk, swore, and then bowed her head and sobbed, while Jake and his brothers wondered what the hell to do to fix this.

Finally, she blew, took a shuddering breath, and sat up straight. She grabbed a fresh tissue and swiped at her eyes. "You are absolutely right. It will be Sadie. As for the other…" Her expression wobbled again. "Damn," she said quietly. "There's so many your dad loved, and yet not enough."

Jake frowned, and a glance showed him similar expressions on his brothers' faces. "What do you mean?" he asked.

"I never imagined he'd be gone so soon. I always

thought we'd both see you boys married. Your wives should be here. Grandbabies should be here."

Jake had barely gotten past the shock of that statement —none of the Walker boys were anywhere close to settling down, let alone becoming rewards members at the baby superstores—when his Mom broke down again.

"Babies always bring comfort during funerals," she cried. "And we don't have any!"

Normally, Rita wasn't the pushy kind of mom. Jake understood that she was grieving and extra emotional right now. In fact, Jake got it entirely. It was way too soon for them to have lost husband, father, and not-yet grandparent Chuck Walker.

2

____

Sadie Evans's shoulders sagged with relief the second she escaped into the kitchen of The Wanderlust to replenish more empty pans of food. Half the city of Pittsburgh seemed to have turned out for Chuck Walker's post-funeral dinner—but there were two men in particular taking up all her air.

One whom she'd always secretly had a serious thing for.

The other, she suspected, was very close to proposing to her. Again.

Sadie shook her head, then dumped the two messy tin pans into the giant garbage can. She was running on fumes at this point. She'd done her share of hugging, crying, consoling, and laughing. Yet she'd held off grieving herself, instead lending her strength to Rita and her energy to preparing for and running this gathering. She'd been working here so long that she didn't know how to just sit and be part of the crowd anyway. That said, she was overdue for a good, honking, ugly cry. She was going to miss Chuck something fierce. He and Rita had employed her for years, but what they'd *really* done was parent her—far better than her own unreliable folks had.

Sadie bit her lip. *Don't cry—just don't. Not yet.*

She hauled open the oven door, grabbed some mitts, and slid a fresh pan of mac and cheese out onto the center counter, and then one of baked ziti.

"Need help?"

Sadie jumped a mile, then spun to glare at Jake Walker.

There you had it. One of the main reasons she was so on edge.

Jake was a maddening, frustrating, ridiculous fantasy she'd harbored since she discovered boys existed. A fantasy she'd thought she'd finally shaken—until he'd shown up last week with his wicked dimple and warm smile and hugged her good and hard. He'd come to be with his mom and help her with the details. Of course he had. He was close to his parents. He was a good person. He was supposed to be here, doing exactly what he was doing.

But *she* wasn't.

She shouldn't have been practically drooling over the man. One look at his stylish suit and the way he filled it out shouldn't have her aching to grab his tie and bring his lips to hers. Her body certainly shouldn't have gone pliant with need after one friendly I-know-you-are-grieving-too embrace from him. What kind of crazy was she that she could think such things when she should be solely focused on missing his dad?

And she most definitely shouldn't still be *here*—in an apron working his parents' restaurant, just like she was when he'd left to live his exciting New York life so many years ago.

"Actually, yes," she managed to reply. She reached over to grab two Sterno cans and a long lighter from across the counter. In her attempt not to step closer to him, she lost her balance and stumbled. When she righted herself, she found she was squeezed between him and the counter —and he had a grip on both her elbows.

A smile twitched one side of his lips, and he raised an eyebrow. "Walk much?"

"Funny," she said, in a decidedly sarcastic tone. She shoved the Sternos and lighter into his chest. "Go replace the ones that ran out."

"You okay, Sades?" he said. One big hand now held the equipment to his chest, but the other smoothed a thumb in a silky caress just above her elbow.

"You bet. Just lots to do, Diner Boy," she said, and slid out of his grasp. The nickname she'd given him when she'd barely had breasts slipped out. Likely it was her subconscious's way of putting him in his place—as a long-ago coworker, a casual buddy she used to rib. A name that had once upon a time reminded her that even though he was the son of the owners, he was no better than her. Just a regular guy.

She shoved his shoulder with her free hand. "Come back for the ziti," she told him.

He held her eyes, and his lips curled into what looked like a satisfied smile. He waited to move until that damn dimple showed up.

What he was satisfied about, she had no idea. The jerkwad.

As the swinging door swooshed behind him, Sadie cursed.

She knew perfectly well that he didn't deserve her ire.

She was angry with herself, ticked off that her heart sped up when he was near, that she'd fallen asleep fantasizing about his lean body sliding over hers, that she still—after all this time—had it bad for him.

And most of all, that he made Tom Radokovich—her perfectly good boyfriend—seem completely unappealing.

———

Jake snuck into the diner's tiny office and shut the door behind him. He scrubbed his hands through his hair and blew out a breath. He loved that so many people had turned out to pay their respects, share their stories, and lament that they'd never have Chuck's perfect Black and Gold Omelet again.

He crossed to the chair behind the desk and huffed out a sad, short laugh. He was pretty sure Kerry Gold cheese and burnt bacon crumbles weren't a state secret—but he got it. He was going to miss his dad too. It wasn't fair. Chuck had been so young—not even sixty-five. But a long-ago virus had weakened his heart. Jake leaned back, swallowed the lump in his throat, and shut his eyes against the tears that threatened.

Minutes later, he heard movement outside, and the approaching voices got louder.

"Let Sadie run it while you take a break." That was Aunt Reenie Zubik, his mom's sister.

"She's due to graduate in June. *Finally.*" The response was from his mom. "I wouldn't ask it of her. Besides, it's too much for one person."

Jake heard the door to the storage room next door open, and the voices became disembodied. Instead of coming through the cheap wooden door, they floated through the duct work and into the office via the vent above his head.

"Sell it! I couldn't!" Rita said. He heard some rustling. She was likely shifting things to get to the stash of booze. Jack Daniel's, tequila, Liquor 43, and some nice wine they hid for special occasions. Without a liquor license, it was only for family after hours.

It was that same stash that was responsible for that kiss with Sadie. That and the private confines of the storeroom. Always that kiss…drawing his mind back, making him touch her earlier when he shouldn't have…

Jake listened closely. If it sounded like his mom and aunt needed any help, he'd abandon his quest for a few minutes of privacy.

"Well," Reenie said, "you can't manage this without Chuck. Like you said, it's too much for one person. I know it's Chuck's legacy, but it's gonna put you in an early grave too if you keep going like this."

Jake cringed. Reenie meant well, but she wasn't exactly full of tact. He didn't hear a response from his mom, but imagined she rolled her eyes and pursed her lips with displeasure—her usual response when Reenie said a little too much.

"It's too bad Jeremy just opened his own place. Ask Jonah to come help. He's not doing much."

"Hah," said Rita. "You know as well as I do, my Jonah plays spin the wheel when he's delivering food."

Jake chuckled. It was true, but he had no idea if Jonah did it on purpose for kicks or simply couldn't be bothered to remember who ordered what.

"What about Jake?" Reenie asked.

"Hah. He was always more like me," Rita said, and Jake smiled at the fondness in her voice. "My Jake had a thirst for travel and an urge to bust out of here from an early age. The minute we'd get back from vacation, he'd start asking where we'd go on the next trip." She laughed. "Remember his face when he first saw Times Square?"

Jake couldn't deny it. When he was younger, he'd ached to experience the wider world. He sucked at languages, but he'd studied abroad in London, backpacked until he'd run out of money, and then interned in Geneva. Offered a job as a result, he'd returned there after graduation. Except he'd only been in Geneva a few months when he was offered something he couldn't turn down in New York. He had always *loved* New York; his initial childlike delight had only morphed into adult interest. The excitement, the hustle, the always-something-going-on of the big city… These days, however, he longed to avoid the crowds, ignore the grime, and get through his day. He still liked to travel, but he couldn't say he had an interest in living abroad right now.

"Yes," Reenie said, "but he was also a natural in this place."

"Enough," said Rita. "Maybe I just wasn't meant to see the world. But I know for sure that my boys need to live their lives. They don't need to be saddled with me and all this. They haven't even found wives yet. And this place should be run by a couple who's already committed—or a pair of siblings or something. Someone with ties."

"A gay couple would be perfect," Reenie exclaimed. "What about those cuties who come in on Sundays? The ones who are buying one of those new condos?"

"Reenie, you have got to stop," Rita said sharply. "I

literally *just* buried Chuck. I'm not selling or passing on the reins anytime soon. End of discussion."

Jake heard the clinking of bottles, and then his mom told Reenie, "Grab a sleeve of the clear tumblers from that box there."

The door slammed behind them, but all Jake could hear was that one question playing over and over in his head.

What about Jake?

He sat up in slow motion and gripped the arms of the chair.

What about Jake?

Whoa.

What about Jake…

What if… Nah… Yes… Well, maybe…

Jake's thoughts spun.

It'd only been two weeks since that team-building trip to True Springs. He'd missed a few days of work to be with his mom and help her contend with all the planning. But because they hadn't held the funeral immediately, he'd returned to his job in between.

That visit to True Springs had loosened something in him. He'd no longer been able to trudge through his workday with blinders on. With eyes wide open, he'd realized he could no longer sit tight, biding his time to figure out how to get out of this particular job and company, and probably out of this career and New York City, too.

Trouble was that he hadn't come up with any answers. He tried to give himself a break, as grieving made it somewhat hard to focus, but still, he'd become more miserable by the day.

Life was too short to waste time doing something that made you unhappy—a fact that wedged itself into your brain like a spike when your dad died unexpectedly of a heart attack.

Exactly what his aunt had been trying to say. Everybody knew his mom wanted to see the world. She'd double-majored in Spanish and French in college. She had stacks of travel magazines and cruise brochures—both in the restaurant and at home. She made anybody who'd come back from a trip tell her every detail, and loved when they brought her a photo to tack on the board she kept on one wall. The story went that she and his dad had planned to grow the diner into a successful establishment and then sell it and travel the world on the buyout earnings. Dad had even named the place The Wanderlust as a promise to his wife.

But Jake figured with kids, making a living, college tuition, health issues, and whatever, they just got stuck in the routine. It was human nature: people got stuck.

Like him.

Jake believed that, unlike him, his parents had been satisfied with their choices, fairly content in their stuck. His dad loved the old place, fed on the buzz and stress of a rush in the kitchen, and became downright gleeful when a newcomer praised his food on Trip Advisor or Yelp. He'd commit bits of the review to memory and sing it at the top of his lungs into a spatula. And his mom had created a warm atmosphere where every patron felt at home and cared for. She made dear friends of all the regulars and family of all the staff.

Like Sadie.

God, it'd been good to see her again. She was more beautiful than ever. What was she now? Twenty-five to his twenty-eight. She'd definitely matured, yet there was an underlying sadness he sensed. He'd always admired her. He knew she worked days at the Children's Museum in programming and her nights and weekends at The Wanderlust, and his mom had mentioned that she'd finally be graduating this semester. Good for her.

If she hadn't been that much younger—in high school when he was in college, in college when he'd landed in New York—they might have actually dated. They might have gone to the movies or parties as a couple, and, of course, they would have stolen far more kisses and copped feels in the storeroom. There'd always been something easy and comfortable between them, which bordered on attraction—but even beyond the age difference, she was a little too close to home. Like a sister or cousin—or exactly what she was: an employee in his parents' diner. And that was exactly what had stopped the one kiss.

Jake thought back. As he recalled, summer had been nearly over, and he'd broken up with his summer girlfriend a couple of weeks before because he'd be spending his senior fall studying in London. Way too far away to consider continuing the relationship. One night at the diner, after shift and before going out, he and his brothers and Sadie had snuck into the storeroom for a couple of shots. But Jonah and Jeremy had taken off fast. He and Sadie were headed to different places but had gotten talking. They sat shoulder to shoulder on the linoleum and passed a bottle of Firefly back and forth. When they finally got up, she lost her balance.

He reached out to steady her, and she hopped on one foot under his hands.

"Ow, ow, my leg's asleep," she said, laughing up at him.

"You're just drunk," he teased.

"I'll admit to tipsy, since I didn't notice my leg, but not drunk." She made a face.

He snorted. It was so Sadie—full of spunk and spit and practicality. And it made him notice her lips.

"Jake?" she asked.

He'd been staring at her, at those big eyes that always shone, those straight teeth with that one crooked one that only made an appearance when she really laughed, the pink lips that had to feel as soft as flower petals, and the brown skin that he just knew would feel warm and silky to the touch.

She hitched in a breath—as if she'd realized where his head was.

He released her arms, only to cup her head. He breathed her in, then kissed her. Her lips softened. Then she melted into him, slid her hands around his back, and pressed him closer.

She felt so unbelievably... There weren't words. He felt—whoa—like never before.

The kiss turned hot, and next thing he knew, he'd pushed her against the rough wood of a built-in and was grinding against her. Her hands were on his skin, roaming under his shirt, up his sides.

She moaned.

"*Jesus*, Sadie."

Sadie.

Wait.

He pulled back with what little willpower he had left.

This was Sadie—now wide-eyed and swollen-lipped and panting.

Holy shit. He shouldn't be kissing Sadie. He *couldn't*

be kissing Sadie. He was leaving. Next week. And next summer he wasn't going to be back, because right after graduation he'd be aiming for New York. And she'd still be here, in school. She would be here for a long time. She was going to attend school here in Pittsburgh, starting as a freshman. She was—*crap*, like one of the family. His family *adored* her—treated her like the missing sister puzzle piece in a family of boys. His older brother Jeremy would call Jake a maggot and beat him to a pulp, that much easier for his dad to skin him alive.

Sadie blinked. The fog of passion disappearing under the same bucket of water that had doused him—only it didn't stop him from wanting her. It only stopped him from acting on it.

Tears welled in her eyes, and hurt seared him as fast as catching a knuckle on the griddle.

"Sadie, I'm sorry—"

But she slipped out of his arms, breaking contact. "Who's calling who drunk, Diner Boy? Jeez."

She bolted out of the storeroom and didn't look back.

Jake let her go. He consoled himself because he'd done the right thing after doing the wrong thing—even though there wasn't a single thing that felt right about that.

Now, Jake rubbed a hand over his eyes, stunned by how clear that memory was. Probably because he was sitting in the diner and he'd been in close proximity to Sadie most of the weekend.

He got up to pace, even though there was only about eight feet of non-linear floor space in this tiny office.

Sadie was *still* here in Pittsburgh. Still a student at Duquesne University. Still working at The Wanderlust. Was she stuck, too?

Aunt Reenie had a point. If his mom didn't go now—travel and experience the world while she still had her health and energy—when would she?

She didn't want to sell. And she wasn't willing to foist the diner onto one person.

What if he could give her that gift? The gift of freedom? Of travel? And let her hang on to the diner—her home base—too?

If he quit his job, sublet or even sold his apartment, and came home and ran this place—

Jake looked around at his parents' office. Old wood paneling on the walls. Framed pictures of he and his brothers on the bookshelf. Binder after binder of tax returns and records… From out front, he could discern voices and laughter from his family and his parents' longtime friends that still gathered. The kitchen was quiet now, but he could hear in his mind the daily clanging and sizzle and shouting, and could practically smell the sweet waft of pancakes and the heavier scent of bacon. His belly was full of the comfort food they'd churned out today. Far more than the house he'd been raised in, the diner meant home.

The family legacy. If he wanted it.

"What do you think, Dad?" Jake murmured, looking at a picture of his dad from two decades ago. He wore a long mustache, a big smile, a Wanderlust apron, and held up a greasy spatula like a microphone. His dad had felt joy here. Not every minute, of course. Owning a small business could be stressful. But overall—the man had been happy. His had been a life well lived.

Would Jake feel that way too? Or would he feel saddled, as his mom had said?

When he'd arrived on Thursday, he'd felt comforted.

At home. Right. Despite mourning his dad, he had been relieved to return. Even now, after a tough couple of days emotionally, it didn't feel constraining—it felt liberating. Like putting on his running shoes after wearing laced-tight, flat-soled dress shoes.

Okaaay, so now he sounded like a commercial for footwear.

It crossed his mind that if he lived here, he'd be in close proximity to Sadie almost daily. And the age difference no longer mattered. Three years only mattered in school. For adults, it was nothing. Then again, Sadie was still part of his family—maybe more so with the additional passage of time.

Jake tried to think ahead, about what daily life might be like here in Pittsburgh, specifically taking on his dad's role at the diner. Maybe—if he could get Rita to travel—both their roles... Not week one, or month one, but after six months or a year? Would he still feel liberated after endless days of grilling, cleaning, serving, ordering, accounting, and payroll? Doubtful.

But satisfied? Proud? Complete?

Man, it was hard to say. But he was pretty damn sure it would feel great to walk away from trading and New York.

And to walk into a place that *meant* something.

3

T he crowd had thinned to family and very old friends, and they'd gotten into the liquor. Sadie had even downed a shot of tequila herself, closing her eyes and focusing only on the tang of the salt and the pull of the lime afterward. Sadie counted as family, but she couldn't stay any longer. She was as overdone as a hash brown that had gotten loose and gone multiple rounds in the fryer.

Rita was sitting between her sister and a cousin, so Sadie squeezed her shoulder. Rita patted her hand.

"The kitchen's clean, and I replenished the desserts," Sadie said. "All you have to do is stick what's left over in the fridge."

Rita wriggled out of her seat and stood. "Why does it sound like you are leaving? You should stay. You know you belong here with us."

Sadie smiled. "I know. But I'm toast." She felt Jake's eyes on her from the other end of the table, but kept her focus on Rita, who also looked tired, but not teary. Oh,

Sadie knew the woman had her moments, but overall she seemed to be a pillar of strength.

"You holding up okay?" Rita asked.

Grief and exhaustion, mingled with the uncomfortable and undeniable yearning she felt for Jake, made Sadie feel like she was on the edge of falling apart. But she said, "Yeah. You?"

"It's good to have all my people together." Rita waved a hand toward her sister, Chuck's siblings, longtime friends, and, of course, her boys.

Sadie couldn't help it. Her gaze locked with Jake's. He'd disappeared for a while earlier, and now there was something different in his eyes. What was it? Speculation? Excitement? Mischief? Trouble? She caught herself frowning and looked away. Whatever it was, it seemed out of place.

Rita gave her a big, rocking squeeze. "Safe trip home," she said. "See you tomorrow."

"Okay. Hope you get some good sleep," Sadie told her. Then she went through the kitchen and out the back, only to find her boyfriend Tom leaning against the railing on the steps of the cement dock.

"Hey," she said. "You didn't have to wait." He'd been at the funeral and the diner, but hadn't overstayed, since he didn't know the Walkers that well.

"I didn't. Went home and then came back. Didn't want you to be alone." He gave her a hug, but she didn't prolong it.

"Thanks," she said.

He didn't ask, just unlocked her bike from the railing and carried it down onto the street next to his, which was propped there. The diner—and much of these few blocks of buildings—was raised above ground level, having once been a warehouse. The area used to feel almost seedy, but the Strip had undergone gentrification that kept on going. Now it was a perfect mix of authentic grittiness and exciting modern amenities for living, dining, and shopping.

Rather than drive, Tom must have biked back just to keep her company on the way home. Good thing, because if he'd been on foot and she'd had to push her bike it would have taken forever. Bone tired, she was glad for his forethought. They crossed the 16th Street Bridge, rode along the river on the North Shore Trail before cutting through downtown, and then took the 9th Street Bridge and entered Allegheny Commons Park. Her neighborhood, the Mexican War Streets, bordered the park on the north. It was a dense neighborhood of eighteenth-century two- and three-story row houses, now mostly beautifully restored, with tree-lined streets and cars usually parked nose to tail along it.

Sadie rented a second-floor apartment from a couple who needed the extra income. When they hopped off their bikes in front of her place, Tom said, "Really makes you think, doesn't it?"

"Hmmn?" Sadie asked as she clipped her helmet onto her bike.

She'd been thinking of how stunning Jake looked in his dark suit and crisp blue shirt, with his warm brown eyes set off above dark scruff. Guilt lodged in Sadie's chest as she pulled herself into the present. Tom—kind, thoughtful, reliable, caring Tom.

"Chuck dying and all," Tom said. "It was so unexpected. It reminds you of how short life is."

"That it does," Sadie murmured, but she suddenly had a bad feeling about where he was going with this, about why he'd come to escort her home. *Not tonight, please,* she thought.

Tom propped his bike against a tree, and then took her free hand in both of his. Her other hand kept a death grip on her handlebars.

She bit her lip and shook her head.

"You keep putting me off," he said.

"I don't want to talk about this tonight of all nights," she said, and meant it with every fiber of her being. But then, she never did want to talk about it, did she?

"It's actually the perfect time, Sadie." He looked sad, even though he wore a small smile. "Circle of life and all that. We should just do it. We fit well together, and I don't see any reason to wait to get married."

She opened her mouth, but he put a finger over her lips.

"Just think about it overnight. Please." He leaned in and gave her a gentle kiss on the lips. "We'll talk tomorrow."

He flipped his bike around, hopped on, and began to pedal away. But she couldn't let him go. Just couldn't keep doing this.

She ran after him. "Tom," she called. He stopped, feet on solid ground and bike between his legs as he twisted to look at her. When she came alongside him, the hope on his face broke her heart. *No more. No more.*

"The answer is no, Tom," she said as firmly as she could, despite the fact that her eyes filled with tears. "And it's not going to change."

A look of shock blanked out his expression.

"You are so good to me. You're an amazing guy," she said. "And I don't know why, I just don't, but it's not right. It's not *everything* between us. It's not what I need or what I always dreamed of. I can't explain it even to myself."

Tom's eyes turned hard and his mouth set like granite. "I see." He nodded once and set his foot to the pedal.

"I'm sorry," Sadie said. "So very—"

His hand shot up to stop her. "You should have told me. A *long* time ago." The words were harsh and clipped with anger. And true, so true.

———

After Sadie had thrown herself on the couch and had a messy sob fest—for poor Tom, for gone Chuck, for widowed Rita, and for her own sorry self—she forced herself into a hot shower. Afterward, she donned her most comfortable knit pajama pants, her softest old Steelers t-shirt, and her fuzziest socks.

She felt rotten about leading on Tom. Not that she'd been *purposely* leading him on. They had fun together. She *liked* him. A lot. She even sometimes loved him. How could you *not* love a person who was so good to you? But sadly, she just didn't feel totally gaga over him. And she could barely explain why to herself, let alone him.

She padded into the kitchen, poured a glass of milk, and dug out the Oreos. Comfort food. And hey, she had only eaten the graham cracker crust bits from the cheese-cake plate when she'd refilled the desserts at The Wanderlust.

She stood at the counter, dunked, and munched as she contemplated.

Everyone thought she should have some grand plan after graduation. But she still didn't have one—or, at least, hadn't committed to one entirely. Much like with Tom, she'd been spinning her wheels.

Sadie blew out a breath, forced herself to seal the cookies, and put them back in the cupboard out of sight.

Her friend Lilian Richter had gone off after college and taught English to kids in Thailand. And she swore it had opened her eyes, changed her outlook, and been the best experience of her life.

So, Sadie had looked into the various programs, and had taken the Teaching English as a Foreign Language course. She'd fit in the hours like it was just another college class, figuring it would give her options. She was double-majoring in elementary education and marketing, because at some point she'd realized she didn't want to be in the classroom long-term. This teaching abroad thing was more about expanding her horizons, boldly grabbing an opportunity to detour, and being open about what might come of it.

Once she'd gotten her TEFL accreditation, she'd ranked her choices (safest for women, best paying, and her own interest level), and then, like magic, she'd gotten offers for multiple interviews from her top choices: South Korea, Thailand, China, and Japan.

Now she had offers in her email inbox just waiting. Although Sadie had been a little hesitant, it seemed like it was meant to be. All she had to do was accept one.

Accepting was what she probably needed. A reset button. A fresh perspective. A surefire way to force her to do something, take some action.

But it'd mean leaving her job at the Children's

Museum. She'd started as an intern four years ago, and now she was the assistant director of programming. And she loved it. It was exactly what she wanted to do.

And the diner. Leaving The Wanderlust would be like leaving home—the home she never had.

If working abroad *didn't* change her life, would her jobs still be here? Sadie bit her lip. They'd have to hire someone else at the museum. Yes, teaching abroad would look good on a résumé, but the Children's Museum couldn't just kick someone else out if Sadie returned to scratch at the door like a stray cat.

Of course, Rita *would* hire her back, even if she had found good help. Sadie wondered if it'd feel the same after such a long absence, though. Already Chuck was gone. Would Rita even want to run it alone—especially if her right hand Sadie left? And for how long?

Sadie wasn't especially excited about the thought of leaving. She *liked* her life.

After seeing Jake this weekend, though, she had to wonder. Had she been biding time here—*waiting* for him? Subconsciously? All these years? When he only came home once in a while? When he'd built a life and a career in New York? When one day, he'd go ahead and marry one of those girlfriends she'd heard about through Rita?

She wouldn't have thought so, but *jeez*…

The way he made her *feel*, just by walking into a room, or smiling at her, or a hint of concern in his eyes… Not to mention that simple caress of her elbow. It was the first time he'd actually touched her in years—and it had brought her crashing back to that magical, earth-shattering encounter in the storeroom all those years ago.

That one touch, that vivid memory—and everyone else

in between vanished like mist in a gust of wind. Because no other man's kisses had ever made her feel that blown away and that whole all at once.

Sadie gripped the counter with both hands.

Dammit. Now that she'd seen him again, she couldn't deny it. She *had* been waiting for Jake. All this time. In vain.

With a wince, she remembered the sliver of hope that had crept into her heart every December and every May. Because Jake had always managed to call it off with some college girlfriend just before his breaks and arrive home single. In no time, he'd find a summer girl, then break up with her, too, as a new semester loomed. He was the leaving type, always looking forward to the next adventure, never stopping long enough to waste effort on the past. Round and round it went every year, every season.

And every season, Sadie would glue that little broken bit of hope back together, only to have it fracture along the same line again.

Because, single or not, in all those months home, Jake had never—not since that one and only kiss—shown her any indication that he cared for her at all beyond basic friendship.

To him, it had been a mistake—something he'd been sorry for. In fact, he'd largely avoided being alone with her ever since, probably because of guilt.

To her, it had been everything.

Would she ever be able to say a wholehearted yes to a great guy like Tom, if she was forever waiting for a guy who'd never given her a real chance? And who likely never would?

Sadie spun out of the kitchen and plopped herself down at the computer.

She clicked open the email from the recruiter, hit reply, and typed: *I'm so pleased to accept the position. Thank you for the opportunity, and I look forward to speaking with you about the details.*

Sadie added her name. She hovered the pointer over the send button…

She shut her eyes, took a deep breath, and clicked.

It was done.

Immediately, she had the urge to toss her cookies right up.

4

J ake was waiting out back on the cement dock behind The Wanderlust when Sadie showed up for her shift Sunday afternoon. She flipped one gorgeous long leg over her bike—the mini-jean skirt showing it off nicely— and cruised to a stop on only one pedal.

The absolute surety he was doing the right thing took a hit from a sudden case of nerves as he looked down at her from the old dock area. It was only a business partnership, sure. But Sadie was his best bet. Maybe his only hope. He couldn't think of anyone else suitable—certainly not anyone else he'd enjoy having by his side every day. What if he couldn't talk her into it? What if she out-and-out refused? Hell, knowing Sadie, there was a really good chance she'd put him in his place and laugh while doing it.

"Hey, Jake."

She glanced at him and hefted her bike up the short set of steps before he managed to offer to help. Then, she removed her helmet and locked up the bike where the railing ended. She'd been using that spot so long that it might have been engraved with her name. Jake watched as she fluffed her hair, unhooked her backpack from the flat rack above the rear wheel, and finally turned her attention on him.

One look at her, two words, three seconds, and he felt a tightening of his skin, an awareness sliding over him, a frisson of pleasure—and then *wham*.

An idea exploded in his brain with no warning. A *better* idea than he'd had initially. What if... *Jesus,* he thought, *again with the what ifs*, yet he couldn't shake the thought...

He'd been planning to ask Sadie to partner with him, to commit, just as he was going to, to running the diner. A business partnership. But what if...

"Headed home?" She eyed the duffel and backpack that sat against the restaurant's back wall.

"Yeah," he said. His brain scrambled, hitting overdrive as the smooth partnership speech he'd prepared disappeared from his memory bank. Snippets of recent conversations darted through his consciousness with lightning speed. His mom's words to Aunt Reenie: a committed couple. His dad gone too soon. His mom still so young and energetic. Her desire for grandbabies.

She smiled. "Where's Rita? Isn't she taking you to the airport?"

"I called a car."

"Ooh, very fancy, Diner Boy."

He didn't sense any malice in the teasing. Given that he was still too occupied with the thoughts darting like bullets through his brain to actually speak, she was probably just trying to fill the space.

For all his mom's coolness, she was very traditional in

some ways. Marriage would give her hope. And hope of grandbabies would serve to really press his timetable. Also, the best marriages were built on solid respect and friendship— *Wait, don't get ahead of yourself.*

"Well, safe trip," Sadie said, and reached for the door.

Come on, Walker, what's the worst that could happen? He was a risk taker by nature, but partnering hadn't seemed so risky. Asking her to marry him—even for practical reasons—whoa.

Jake blurted out, "Hold up—I wanted to talk to you about something important."

Sadie raised an eyebrow but let go of the door and turned to face him. "Okaaay. I'm listening."

And wow, having her full attention, he realized he wanted this. Badly. What did that mean, exactly? Mentally, he shook his head. Maybe not all his reasons were practical ones, but he'd sort that later and go for it now. He'd have to wing it, but it was worth a shot. And there was always plan B (the boring business partnership)—not that he'd tell Sadie that.

She tapped a foot.

Jake jump-started his mouth. "I've been doing a lot of thinking. I want to help my mom out. And to really make my plan work, I need your help."

"You know I'll be here helping her more than ever before, right?" she asked. She looked at him askance, like he had forgotten how much Sadie loved his mom or how great she herself was.

Uh, yeah, not a chance. Those were two key elements here.

Jake shook his head. "It's way bigger than that. I'm going to come home and take over so she can travel—

while she's still young and healthy—just like she's always wanted to."

Sadie's eyes popped open wide. "You'd leave New York to come home and run the diner?"

"Yes. I don't have a doubt in my mind that it's the right thing to do."

"Wow," Sadie said, shaking her head. "That's really big of you. But I don't think she'd want you to leave your job, your life, for her… She's really strong. She's—"

"It's not just for her. It's for me. And hopefully it will be a good thing for you, too."

Sadie narrowed her eyes and crossed her arms over her chest. "I'm getting a bad feeling about how this involves me."

———

Sadie's mind raced. Was Jake trying to fire her? Ahead of coming home? Or was he aiming to enlist her as some sort of spokesperson on his behalf? Neither of those things made sense, but she wasn't coming up with anything that did.

And what in the world made him think Rita would want him to drop everything to come back here? The woman adored her boys and wished she saw them all more often, but she wouldn't want him sacrificing himself. Sadie eyed him closely. He *looked* like grown-up, successful Jake. He was standing tall and fit in a long-sleeved pullover and sweats and running shoes—a getup that only enhanced his lean gorgeousness. Hot as ever, unfortunately for her.

"Hear me out," Jake said. "You know how Mom's

always wanted to travel, right? Once they'd sold the diner, they planned to see the world. Dad's promise to her."

Sadie waved a hand impatiently.

"Well, if I come home," he said, lifting a shoulder and then dropping it, "she can go."

"Yeah, right," Sadie said, relaxing a little as she realized he didn't have a plate to put whatever crazy concoction this was on, "only she still won't go."

"Exactly," Jake said with a big smile. "She believes it's too much for one person."

"Because it is." Normally Jake was a smart guy, but she wasn't seeing any logic coming her way. She hoisted her backpack up further on her shoulder.

"But if two people were committed to running it together?" Jake raised his eyebrows, suggesting…

Suggesting what? "Are you offering me some kind of partnership? Just spit it out already." She didn't have time for this, and he was cracked if he thought she had any kind of capital for some kind of family-ruining buyout. "I'm going to be late."

"No—it's bigger than that." Jake sucked in a big breath. "I'm asking you to marry me."

Sadie's mouth dropped open. Her heart stuttered with shock and then recovered, as if Cinderella's pumpkin carriage had appeared and then vanished all in the space of a second.

She barked out a laugh—because really, what other way was there to react? "You are out of your mind."

"I'm completely serious."

She scrunched up her face and peered at him. His hair was mussed, but his eyes were clear and he wasn't muttering or drooling or frothing. Not drugs, not a psychotic episode, not even sleepwalking.

And sadly, most definitely *not* some romantic notion blown out of proportion as a result of one heart-stopping kiss seven years ago.

She asked, "What in the world would that accomplish?"

He ran a hand through his hair, disheveling it further. "I don't think my mom is going to believe that I really want this—coming home and running the diner. I think she'll expect me to bail."

Sadie snorted. "Duh. You're Mr. Travel, Mr. Big City, Mr. Fancy Career, Mr. Next Big Thing—"

"Enough," Jake said.

"But my next one was really good," she said.

Jake rolled his eyes and fought a smile. "That's just it," he said. "But if I had a *reason* to stay. If I *committed* to a reason to stay…"

"A wife," she muttered, shaking her head.

"I know it seems far-fetched," Jake said. "But it could work. It'd be a practical thing. I'm not asking you to make it a forever marriage."

Even given how cracked this conversation was, Sadie's heart took a serious punch at that. She had to force herself not to react.

"I'm thinking we elope. City hall or Vegas or something. Then you give me six months. At max. If all goes well, it won't even take that long for my mom to go. I'm going to buy her a serious travel itinerary as a surprise and enlist Aunt Reenie as a travel companion. I just—she has to feel it's real, that *I'm* for real, or she'll never be comfortable leaving. And she has to have some sense of urgency. If we're married, she'll be expecting grandchildren before long—"

Sadie's eyes must have bugged out, because he held up a hand.

"Hang on," he said. "I'm not saying we'd be actually giving her any, just that the idea of it will force her to take the trip, not keep putting it off. She'd never want to go anywhere again if there were babies on the scene."

Sadie stared at him, trying to see if he had sprouted a third head or had a giant bump responsible for this insanity. Mainly, trying to process the fact that yes, Jake was actually serious.

Jake took a step forward. "There's something in it for you, too. Name your price."

Involuntarily, her mouth twisted and she took a step back.

"No," Jake added, "don't take that the wrong way. It wouldn't be like that. And you certainly don't have to sleep with me or kiss me—" Jake visibly gulped.

This conversation just got worse and worse, Sadie thought with horrified wonder. He sucked at persuasion—even for practical purposes.

He continued, "I just thought I could help you. I know it's taken you a long time to get through school because you were paying your own way. I could pay off your loans or give you a nest egg to go wherever or start whatever after graduation. I want to do something good for you, too."

"Holy shit, Diner Boy, this is just… Wow. There aren't words."

"It's a lot to take in, I know," he said. "But I'm dead serious. I'm coming home either way. But I really want to do this for my mom, and I don't see that she will ever fulfill that dream if I don't force it to happen."

He searched her face, then shoved his hands in his pants pockets.

"Take the week and think about it. I'll be back next weekend," he said. "Tell me your answer then."

5

———————

That week, Sadie spent her days at the Children's Museum half focused on work, while rehashing every word Jake had said. Partly to convince herself that she hadn't really just accepted a two-year position in Gumi, South Korea, starting only four months from now—the very night before Jake Walker had asked her to marry him. Partly to convince herself that conversation had actually happened. Because she'd dreamed of that day—like an idiot—for years.

Granted, that odd convo was hardly the stuff dreams were made of. In fact, it was so craptastic that it might have been one of the worst proposals in history. Fine, fine, his motives came from the heart, even if they were misguidedly macho and uber-controlling. And *crazy*.

She spent her evenings either daydreaming through class or mixing up drink orders and forgetting sides at the diner. What would it be like to waitress day in and day out in the same tight space as Jake? Because he'd said that he was coming home either way.

And later, when she was supposedly doing her part on her last group project for her last marketing course, she went round after round dissecting every reason why this lunatic idea of his was doomed to fail epically. Yet she couldn't help thinking of ways to make his plan better.

Jake had already texted her with his arrival time, which happened to coincide with her day off and the Pirates' home opener at PNC Park. Chuck and Rita were season ticket holders, but often Sadie or one of their boys was asked to come along or even just take the tickets—especially if Rita didn't want to brave the rain. This time, Rita had told Sadie to take a friend, because she wasn't ready yet to go sit there without Chuck.

Sadie had been thinking a lot about Rita, and even what Chuck would think of Jake's plan. And she'd come to the conclusion that Chuck would probably approve. At the very least, he'd like her proposal better than Jake's. So she told Jake to meet her at the game and left his ticket at will call.

On Sunday afternoon, she settled in for the first inning wearing her lucky t-shirt, a black windbreaker, her boyfriend-style ripped jeans, and her black ball cap with the gold P. It was a gorgeous evening. The early spring weather was cool and crisp, the sunset over the city was perfection, and the stunning view of the city made all things seem possible.

She wasn't sure if she was nervous at seeing Jake again, or nervous that he'd say yes instead of no…but this was one of her happy places, and as the game ramped up, she forgot to worry.

The Pirates were up by the hair on their chins, and

soon she was hooting and hollering and groaning along with all the other fans.

At the top of the fifth, Jake slid into the seat next to her. She hadn't seen him coming and nearly choked on a chunk of hot pretzel.

He pounded on her back until she held up a hand.

"Okay now?"

She nodded and sucked some pop. "Yes," she said, then took a napkin to her watering eyes.

"So what have I missed?" Jake asked.

Sadie cleared her throat one last time and handed him the hot pretzel.

"Thanks," he said. "I haven't eaten since breakfast."

Sadie waved him off and then caught him up. "Cuba Zaynia got caught stealing, Big Ry Guy can't hit for shit as usual, and the Cardinals are obviously not going down easy tonight." All the while, she was wondering why he always had to look so good.

"I see you still follow closely," Jake said with a wink.

He watched a few plays, but Sadie caught him looking around the stadium.

When the inning switched over, he asked, "My mom didn't want to come, huh?"

"She said she wasn't ready."

"She could wait years, and it would still feel like he should be here," Jake said.

Sadie nodded. "Chuck loved all this. They saw how many games together, you think?"

Jake leaned back. "They had tickets since before my brothers and I were born, so probably over thirty seasons' worth?"

"Wow," she said.

During the seventh-inning stretch, nearly everyone in earshot got up to wander or grab food.

Jake angled his body to face her. "So," Jake said, "you've had some time to think."

Sadie adjusted her cap and fought the urge to pull it low and hide under the brim. Instead, she dropped her legs from the chair in front of her and sat up straight.

———

All week, Jake had wondered if he'd overplayed his hand, should have offered the partnership instead. He could always have schmoozed her into the practical marriage idea later. And now? Damn. Sadie looked so serious that Jake's hopes took a nosedive right out of the stadium seats.

Only when she looked him in the eye and opened her mouth, the word that came out was "Yes."

Jake jumped up, pumped a fist with an emphatic *yes*, then pulled her to her feet and hugged her.

"Hang on there, Diner Boy." She laughed, but pulled away in an uncharacteristic show of nervousness. "It's only a yes if you meet my conditions."

"Oh, okay," Jake said. He was still elated. Yes was yes. He could deal with whatever else. A certain amount of money? An exotic honeymoon? A curtain dividing the bedroom? Dibs on the streaming choices? "Like what?"

"Here's the thing." She looked out at the now-dark sky. "I get that you want to do this for your mom, and maybe now that you've made up *your* mind, you're all fired up and rearing to go. But we can't just elope or make some big announcement right away."

Jake braced himself.

Sadie continued, "The funeral last weekend was the most time we've spent together in years. And Rita knows I'm way too practical to run off and do some drunken-elopement night, Vegas-style. She won't believe it. Jeez, she'd probably march us down to the City-County Building and demand we get the thing annulled. And then she'd be so spitting mad, she'd flat-out refuse to leave."

Jake's hopes wobbled precariously again. She was right. Duh.

Sadie took a deep breath. "Furthermore, she'd never forgive us—and I can't bear that."

He heard a quiver in her voice. Rita was his mom, of course, but for all intents and purposes, she'd been that to Sadie, too. He felt a stab of regret for even asking her to lie.

"So what I'm saying is, go ahead and announce your plans to stay, and then court me for a month or six weeks." Sadie's eyes slid away, and a blush rose on her cheeks. "A whirlwind romance like that, she might just buy, given that we've known each other forever."

"You're brilliant," he said, and smiled. Even six weeks would barely change anything. "And you're right on all counts. One hundred percent."

She nodded, looking a little shell-shocked. "One more thing."

"What is it?"

"I don't want to go to Vegas. I want to"—Sadie gulped visibly—"get married downtown."

He nodded. "Fine."

"With your mom in attendance."

Jake reared back. *That*, he didn't like. That would be

like lying straight to Rita's face—when he'd imagined all this subterfuge perpetrated behind closed doors. "I don't know about that part."

Sadie nodded. All serious. "I won't do it otherwise. So take it or leave it."

6

S adie showed up for her shift Tuesday night, knowing Jake was already there because Rita had texted yesterday to let her know the good news: Jake was home to stay and he'd be helping out at The Wanderlust. Of course, Sadie had acted surprised—no big stretch, since she was practically still in shock herself.

Rita had to be over the moon, and this was a good thing for the Walker family. But Sadie worried. Was Jake really here to stay? She doubted it. Oh, he might *think* this was what he wanted, but it'd been a long time since he'd lived this life. For all Pittsburgh was a sizable, dynamic city with so much to offer, it still managed to feel like a small town with a Midwest mindset and a working-class attitude. Especially when you narrowed down to the Strip, despite the recent gentrification. And even more so if you went by the microcosm of The Wanderlust.

And Jake was a big-city guy who'd always itched to get *out*. He practically lived for vacations and trips. He'd gone away to college, he'd studied abroad, he'd interned abroad, and then he lived for years in the most exciting (she was going on hearsay here) city in the world: New York City, the Big Apple, the City that Never Sleeps. Whatever you called it, it was a far cry from where he grew up.

She rubbed her forehead—and not because she had a helmet mark from her ride over. When Jake invariably bailed, chances were good that Rita's heart wouldn't be the only one left in pieces.

Sadie fortified herself with a deep breath before she yanked open the door. Sucker that she was, she'd been looking forward to seeing Jake again and practically vibrating with nerves about maybe dating him—pretend or not.

"Hey all," Sadie called as she hung up her backpack and jacket in the set of cupboards by the back door.

As she came through the doorway into the kitchen, Jake grinned—yep, just as devastatingly good looking as he'd been on Sunday—and clicked the grill tongs at her. "I haven't lost it, Sades."

Chuck normally cooked on Benny's nights off, so of course Jake had taken those shifts. He even wore a bandana pirate-style to secure his hair and catch sweat once it got hot, like his dad had done. Of course, his was red and his dad had always chosen something black and gold.

"That right?" she asked. "Do the regulars agree?"

"No complaints last night," Rita said with a smile. Then she leaned toward Sadie and said behind her hand, "He's got some big boots to fill, though."

Her eyes glistened with emotion, so Sadie squeezed her hand. "He sure does."

Rita bustled away toward the storeroom. Sadie made quick work of her apron and checked to make sure she had an order pad, a couple of pens, and some straws.

After all the years they'd spent together, this was so normal—and yet so odd all at once.

It might well get weirder once she'd pinned Jake down. Sunday night they'd stayed to watch the end of the game and he'd walked her home. He'd been pensive, so they hadn't chatted much. She'd figured he needed time to think. Tonight, she'd better get an answer. She couldn't stand not knowing: were they on or not?

She glanced over her shoulder at Jake—shaking his head over an order but grinning nonetheless. Her heart did a little flip. Pleasure. Nerves. Hope…

Later, during the lull between the early birds and the evening rush, Jake came out of the kitchen. He raised his arms overhead and stretched, then went to chat up some of the regulars who sat along the back wall.

Sadie smiled and shook her head as she listened. An older couple reminded him about the time he showed off his smarts by practicing his alphabet via a squirt bottle of ketchup. No paper—just the diner floor.

"Caught before I reached the letter K, as I recall," Jake said with amusement in his voice. "Where are Jill and Karen living these days?" he asked the older couple.

That was one of the things Sadie had always liked about Jake. He took time for people. She rolled her eyes at herself. Okay, fine, his killer smile, sexy voice, and great laugh had a lot to do with it.

He was talking with another couple he didn't know as well and asking lots of questions, when she returned with dishes of ice cream for a young mother and her two boys.

They asked for more napkins and some water, so she headed back to the kitchen.

On her second trip back, she crossed paths with Jake—because despite a nearly empty restaurant, he'd chosen the same aisle as she had. He brushed against her with a sexy grin—and all she could think was thank goodness she wasn't delivering the ice cream, because it'd have been a milky puddle.

Sadie delivered the water and napkins, left the check, and let the woman know to holler if she needed anything else. She returned to a bus bin she'd left on a booth in front. She cleared what she could then stretched across the length of the table to retrieve the farthest items, and then she felt a tingle—from the roots of her hair to the tips of her toes.

Sadie snuck a glance over her shoulder, and sure enough, Jake was behind the counter holding a mug of coffee. But it was a prop. In reality, he was just standing there watching her—actually ogling her backside. And yowza, the heat that was in his eyes…

Which meant that not only had he made a decision, he'd already begun the game.

She straightened, hefted the bin, and put a little extra sass in her step. Rather than go to the far end of the counter and enter the kitchen directly, she sidled through the break in the middle of the counter so that this time *she* could brush past *him*.

His eyes widened when she stopped—only slightly deer in the headlights. She smiled with a slow curve of her lips. She thrilled at the prospect of doing this—flirting with him, pouring on the heat, acting out something she'd desired forever…

She wouldn't have started it—but he already had—so she leaned in close and murmured right into his ear. "So we're on, huh, Diner Boy?"

He raised an eyebrow. "Oh, yeah. We're definitely on."

———

On Friday evening, as soon as it started to slow down, Jake sent his mom home.

"You sure, hon?"

"Absolutely," he said. "Even if the last customers stay until closing, Sadie and I still have time to catch Dog Daze's last set over at Jeremy's." By Jeremy's, Jake meant the music club his brother Jeremy owned called Vine (as in "I Heard It Through the Grapevine" like the soul classic). It had quickly become *the* place in Pittsburgh to hear some cutting-edge new bands.

Sadie raised an eyebrow at Jake from across the way where she cleared a table. He'd asked her earlier if she'd go with him, but they'd been in the weeds all night and hadn't had a chance to talk details.

"Oh," Rita said, and looked back and forth between the two of them.

Jake plated some buns and lettuce and tomato for what he hoped was the last order. He wasn't sure if his mom was surprised that he and Sadie planned to hang out, concerned because she'd noticed them flirting this week, or reluctant to let them close the diner up alone.

"We have this, Mom," Jake said. "Go home and take a load off."

"All right, I will," Rita said.

Sadie waved at her and slipped through the swinging doors to the front.

It'd been a long week of emotional ups and downs for them all. He knew being at home without his dad wasn't any better for his mom than being here without him. Still, she had to be exhausted.

As for him, there were counterbalances. He missed his dad, but he was glad to be home and really excited to be on the path to doing something good for his mom.

Then there was Sadie. It'd been one helluva week of flirting with her. What was it about her? They hadn't even needed any warmup time—they'd just started sharing looks and quips, and before he knew it, he could barely keep an order straight because he was so tuned in to her.

Every time she reached across him to slide the order tickets down (he silently thanked his dad for keeping it old school), every time she flashed him that wide grin across the room, every time he managed to get within range of her scent…

He flipped a couple of burgers and tossed some shrimp and stole a glance toward the front, knowing she'd be back looking for this order soon.

He shook his head. He'd thought that because this was a practical arrangement, that they could just act their way through it. Yeah, he'd had the hots for her when he was younger, but he'd spent so many years avoiding her that he'd sort of thought he was in the clear. He'd always believed they were better off as friends. The old reasons still stood: she worked here, she was part of the family. Heck, to his mom? Sadie was the daughter she'd never had. Jake had never wanted to mess with that.

Until now. Now he really, really wanted to mess with that. He was practically obsessed with messing with that.

That was why he'd suggested the show tonight. He'd originally been thinking they'd go out next week, but the heavy flirting had pushed the gas pedal on his timeline. Plus, they might as well start easing his mom into this idea. The sooner they spent time together outside of The Wanderlust, the better.

As far as he was concerned, the more time they spent together period, the better.

He *liked* Sadie. Always had. He liked her enough—and the feeling was mutual, he thought—that they could exit this charade with their friendship intact, right?

He just had to remember to keep his hands to himself tonight.

Or did he?

7

———

S adie got a strange thrill from showing up at Vine with Jake in tow. Her bouncer friend had raised an eyebrow; her bartender friend raised two. Sadie figured Jeremy would do the same once he spotted them—too bad he didn't have three eyebrows. Then again, Jeremy thought of her like a sister and might just as easily assume that it was no different for Jake—that they were simply buddies.

Sadie introduced Jake to the staff she knew, but she had an odd desire to keep him all to herself, so she didn't bother with small talk. Once they each had a beer in hand, she grabbed his hand and tugged him across the space toward the far wall. That was another thrill—holding hands with Jake. She was allowed—even supposed to— touch him because of this arrangement. It felt just right. Totally natural.

They'd arrived between sets, and the interim music was loud, but manageable.

Jake clinked his bottle with hers. "So what's Dog Daze's most well-known song?"

"'Trio', definitely."

"Is that your favorite?"

"They're all good. You'll see."

The band came on and the volume rose exponentially. Sadie grinned at Jake and hollered her support.

Somewhere in the middle of the set, a server with black hair and loads of piercings shouldered up to them with a full tray. She plucked two bottles up and handed them to Jake. "From Jeremy," the server shouted, and inclined her head toward the bar.

Sure enough, Jeremy was over there moving at his usual hundred miles an hour. As soon as he looked toward them, they both raised their drinks. He nodded and held up a hand.

Good timing on the cold brewskies, Sadie thought. Heat rose between her and Jake—and not just from dancing. She'd caught Jake's gaze on her breasts and swinging hips, and she'd been eyeing him up, too. She appreciated a man who could dance. Rhythm and coordination would transfer nicely to the bedroom.

Yowza. Thank goodness the lights were low, because her cheeks were on fire at that thought.

Just then, the lead singer said, "We're gonna slow things down now."

They launched into a sexy blues number—one that was fraught with innuendo and "nothing like some good loving" lyrics. Jake took Sadie's beer from her hand and put it on the narrow ledge along the wall.

"Dance with me," he said. He put his hands on her hips and tugged her close. Sadie raised an eyebrow but couldn't stop the smile that played about her lips. She looped her arms behind his neck, and they moved together.

God, he felt good and smelled good—because yes, she still smelled him, spicy soap and warm male, under the smell of the griddle that felt like home to her. She looked into his face and saw he had to tear his eyes from her lips.

He held her gaze until the song changed into its most soulful part. She loosened her hands, arched her torso backward, and let her head fall back and circle with the music. When she came back upright, he pulled her even closer—right against him—and kept both hands pressed to the small of her back. She wondered if he wished they were on her butt, because she sure did.

She took a deep breath, expanding her chest, and Jake's eyes lingered there and then traveled, heavy-lidded, over her collarbones, her neck, her chin, her lips, before finally meeting her eyes. The heat she saw there shot straight to her core. She felt smokin' and languorous and needy all at once.

He leaned in, and for just a second, she felt his breath on her neck. Then his lips closed over the tendon there. She moaned.

He said into her ear, "*This* is *my* favorite song."

An electric current shot through her body. If they'd been somewhere private, she'd have lifted one leg and wrapped it around him. Truth be told, she might have wrapped *both* legs around him.

The song ended just as Jake straightened. Sadie was gratified to see that his eyes looked as heavy with desire as her body felt.

She wasn't the only one affected. Unless maybe, unlike her, Jake had retained a clear head and was aware that they could feasibly have an audience—his brother.

Maybe he was pretending, pushing fast forward on this script, even here.

———

If it hadn't been for the lights coming up, Jake would have kissed Sadie right there on the dance floor. Watching her dance, then feeling her move—whoa. His body could easily have beat a coal-fired oven for temperature.

As it was, they stayed pressed together, her arms looped over his shoulders, his thumbs at her waist and his fingers on her lower back, reluctant to let her go.

She gave him a sexy smile, and her fingertips moved softly over the short hair at the nape of his neck.

"That song might be my new favorite, too," Sadie said.

He smiled back and rubbed his thumbs over her hipbones, denim and all. "It's good to have an open mind about these things."

Her eyes sparkled and she opened her mouth—

And then some drunken ass rammed into them, breaking them apart.

"Hey, watch it," Jake said. He shoved the guy out of their space, blocking Sadie in the process in case things got crazy. But the dipshit only raised his hands to say sorry and tottered away.

Jake turned back to Sadie, but the spell had been broken.

Even now, walking her home, he couldn't stop thinking about kissing her. He remembered how good she'd felt all those years ago when they'd swigged Firefly in the storeroom and things had gotten a little out of hand. He suspected she'd feel even better now.

Jake looked at her out of the corner of his eye. They'd stopped back at The Wanderlust for her things. He carried her backpack over one shoulder. Although he'd offered, she pushed her bike. He had the distinct feeling that she was using it as a barrier. It wasn't between them, but still, it kept her hands and her focus occupied. Maybe he wasn't the only one that had the urge to touch…

He'd like to be holding her hand right now. He'd like to wrap his arm around her waist and walk in step. More than anything, he'd like to stop in the middle of the street and tilt her face up and taste her gorgeous, full lips…

He'd been so caught up at the bar—the music, her movements, the look in her eyes, and then her sexy body flush against his—that he'd put his lips to her neck during that song. She'd smelled sweet and tasted salty, but it was her moan that had really sent him over the edge.

He wished like hell he knew what she'd been about to say before they were interrupted.

What he did know was that it would have been good. It would have been flirty and sassy and stunning. And probably it would have either stopped his heart or sent it into overdrive.

Because this was Sadie. And this was how he reacted to her.

One long-ago, mind-blowing kiss. One week of flirting culminating in one hot-as-hell dance. And all those years of distance in between didn't mean squat.

The realization hit him as painfully as a frying pan upside the head. He wasn't going to be able to be just friends with Sadie.

He wanted more. He'd wanted his hands all over her, and hers all over him. He wanted—

Shit. What did that mean for him—for them—at the end of all this?

He almost didn't care what it meant. He'd never gone wrong following his instincts. He'd always known what he wanted. Right now he wanted—

No—Jake shook the larger implications off. It was too much to contend with right now. He'd just have to trust his gut and worry about the rest later.

He stole another glance at Sadie. She looked down at her handlebars, the helmet swaying where it hung with each step. Her shoulders looked tense; her gait was stiff. Gone were the fluid, sultry moves from the bar, the sexy smile, the half-lidded eyes.

He had jumped ahead. Dove all in. But she wasn't there with him. Not right this second, anyway.

"Beautiful night," he said.

She glanced at the sky above the buildings and said, "It sure is." But instead of meeting his gaze or even turning her head his way, she refocused dead ahead.

Jake shoved his hands in his pockets. He didn't know what to say or how to bring them back to the easy, connected feeling they'd enjoyed all week. And it was a long walk on foot.

Hell, maybe she was a really, really good actor. Maybe tonight it had been all about the music and the fact that she'd had a little beer at the end of a long week. Maybe he'd misread her entirely and that death grip she had on the bike meant *hey, dude, I agreed to the charade, but don't push it.*

When they reached Sadie's building, she stopped and finally looked at him. "Thanks for tonight," she said. "That was nice."

Jake mimicked stabbing himself in the heart. "Just nice?"

She rolled her eyes. "All right, it was fun."

He grinned. "I can live with that. For now."

She propped a hand on her hip. "What does that mean?"

Jake shrugged—hell, he didn't even know what it meant yet—and handed her backpack over. "Can I carry your bike up?"

"I've got it," she said, and he suspected she didn't want to deal with him inside her apartment. She narrowed her eyes. "What are you cooking up?"

"That's for me to know and you to find out."

"You sound like you're ten years old all over again," she said.

"You didn't know me when I was ten," he said.

"Good thing, too, because I wouldn't have liked you much," she muttered, but Jake knew she was just feigning annoyance.

He leaned in and kissed her softly on the cheek. He hovered close enough that he could smell her and long enough to make sure she'd wonder if he was going to kiss her for real.

"I would have liked you," he said, and looked her right in the eye. "A lot."

Her eyes widened and her lips parted. Jake took a chance and caressed her lower lip with his thumb—though he wished like hell it was his tongue.

Her breath hitched. Satisfied, he felt his lips curl up. He was so damn tempted to lean in, yet he forced himself to turn away. He'd only made it a couple of steps before he remembered one more thing and turned. She hadn't moved, was just standing there staring after him—which was a very, very good sign.

He grinned. "*I* had a *great* time tonight."

8

Sadie and Jake both worked a long shift Saturday. He gave her a brilliant smile when she arrived, and the next thing she knew, he'd drawn her right back to the teasing and flirting she'd so enjoyed the week before.

It wasn't that she didn't want to. Oh, she wanted to, all right.

She'd just gotten nervous last night. Because she realized after that dance just how badly she wanted him. Just how far under his spell she was. Sheesh, if that buffoon hadn't bumped into them, if they'd been anywhere but in public? She'd have jumped into bed with him before she had time to think it through.

Because it all felt so good. So right.

Probably because she'd always wanted this, wanted him. Dreamed of it—yet never dreamed it would *really* happen.

Yet it was happening—and that was the problem. It felt real. At least whenever she was interacting with him. And she desperately wanted it to be real.

But as soon as the evening rush died down and she spent less time rushing for customers and more time on menial tasks like setting tables and restocking things, she had too much time to think.

"Goodnight," she called to some customers who'd already paid but finally decided to stop lingering. She waved as they headed out the front door, then grabbed a bin and bused their table.

She suspected that to Jake, none of their flirting was real. To him, it was probably a plan of action. A carefully thought out charade. She gave him a sidelong glance as she crossed the kitchen. What did he give her in return?

A wink! He was executing his plan like a master. Playing her like a fiddle custom-made for him.

She slammed down the bus bin of dishes on the metal counter way too hard. Sal, the usual dishwasher (not that they didn't all pitch in when need be), raised an eyebrow.

"Sorry," she said.

"Sadie," Rita called from out front.

Sadie hustled out of the kitchen, only to meet Rita behind the counter. "Two parties just came in. One's big. You want them or do you need a break soon?"

"I'll take them both, if Denise is cool with that." It would keep her mind occupied.

"She's hoping to leave early, so all yours."

"Awesome," Sadie said, and went to greet clients and share the specials.

The new tables turned out to be just the beginning of a late-night rush. Despite that, she and Jake somehow ended up in the kitchen alone around eleven p.m. She clipped a ticket up and slid the magnet down toward Jake, whose bandana looked decidedly damp with sweat by now. She turned to go, but Jake snagged a finger in her apron strings and tugged her back.

"What are you thinking so hard about today, Sades?" he asked. He looked earnestly into her eyes.

Crumb. Was she wearing every unsure, worried thought plastered across her face?

"I'm too busy to think." She swatted at his hand. "And you should be too. We've got three more four-tops nearly ready to order."

"Stop thinking," he said, and squeezed her waist between two fingers.

She yelped and squirmed away. Not only was she ticklish, it was the first time he'd touched her today.

George, today's kitchen assistant, returned with an armful of items from the freezer.

Jake leaned into Sadie's space and said in a low voice, "Just enjoy this ride with me." Then he smiled that mischievous grin that always got her. "It's gonna be *way* better than nice. It's going to be *great*."

That was exactly what worried her. Jake had only been home for a week. And they'd gone out once. Yet she was already having the time of her life.

She was totally doomed.

———

Rita insisted that Jake take Sunday off, just like his dad used to, so Jake slept in. He lay in the queen-sized guest bed corner to corner for a while, stretching out his tight muscles. He was in decent shape; he ran and worked out regularly. Standing on his feet and sweating over a hot grill most of the week, however, was a whole different kind of ache.

Before he and Sal had finished up last night, Sadie had called goodbye and slipped out the door. He'd been hoping to escort her home again and maybe steal a late-night kiss, although he would have been happy if she'd just graced him with one of her wide, happy smiles. Instead, it seemed, she'd purposely avoided him, and he had no idea why.

Jake finally levered himself up and padded out to his mom's kitchen. She was putting on her jacket and reaching for her purse.

"Church?" he asked.

"Yes, sir," she said. "You should try it sometime."

He raised an eyebrow and shook his head. This was an old conversation, and he knew she didn't care so much as she liked to pretend she did.

"Plenty to eat in the fridge, if you can stand to cook something."

He gave her a wry grin. "I don't suppose there's any cereal?" He and his brothers had gone through metric tons of the stuff when they were young.

She chuckled. "Bottom shelf of the pantry."

She had to tell him because his parents had downsized to this updated two-bedroom home only a couple of years ago. It was still in Bellevue, but wasn't the old house he'd grown up in.

"There's still coffee in the pot," she said. She headed toward the door.

"Hey, Mom?" he called as he snagged a mug. "Are you planning on going to the game this afternoon?"

She sighed, her shoulders sagging. "I thought about it, but no, I don't think I will."

"When you're ready," he said, "I'll go with you."

She came back into the room and kissed him on the cheek with a big *mwaaa* sound. "You always were my favorite."

"Hah," Jake said. He well knew that whoever was behaving best was her favorite. "Did you promise the tickets to anyone?"

"Nope, they're all yours," she said.

"Good. I'll see if Sadie wants to come."

Rita cocked her head. "You two are spending a lot of time together lately."

He shrugged and played it cool. "We hit Vine on Friday. Jeremy's place is the place to be, and people of the same age group do those things, Mom." He poured coffee, then looked up. "I don't even know if she's free this afternoon. And I can't help it if we work together. Don't read into it."

Better, Jake felt, if his mom thought their relationship was evolving naturally. Friends spending time together leading to oops, we're now kissing. Besides, even if Rita had noticed some flirting at the restaurant, she'd still expect her son to be holding back—especially from his mom.

Rita threw up her hands. "Okay, okay. I'm going."

She left, and Jake took a tentative sip of the hot brew. He grabbed his phone to call Sadie. Then he thought better of it and decided to text.

Sadie had been the one to suggest that he should court her—but now that he'd begun, she was planting stop signs in his path. He didn't want to scare her off by coming on too strong or racing things along, but he found he didn't want to waste time, either. Not because of the master plan, but because he was enjoying being with her. He wanted *more* of being with her.

Hell, he'd admit it. He also couldn't stop fantasizing about getting her in bed. And if Friday night was any indication, they *would* end up in bed. *Before* they ended up at the magistrate.

Friends slept together all the time—that friends-with-benefits thing people did. He'd had a couple of women friends over the years that had evolved into that. Neither he nor they had expected anything more, and they'd retained an easy friendship even when they stopped sleeping together.

Surely, he could manage that with Sadie. Sleeping together, married, *and* friends. Of course, she hadn't agreed to sleeping together—yet—but she had said yes to the practical marriage, after all. She wouldn't have if she thought their friendship would be at risk. That he was sure of. And marriage was a bigger deal than sleeping together.

A ping came back. Jake grinned. Sadie had agreed to go to the game. She might be skittish around him still, but she was nuts about baseball. And he planned to make the most of today.

————

Sadie arrived a little early at the meeting spot she and Jake had agreed on, since he had both the tickets. Probably, she'd walked too fast in her excitement to see him. She tucked herself against a building to stay clear of the throng of people heading toward the stadium and kept an eye out for Jake.

Instead, she spotted Tom. He was about a block down on the other side of the street, and he walked with a young woman. She had generous curves, blond hair cut to chin length, and oversized sunglasses. Best of all, she wore a happy smile as she gazed up at Tom. In turn, his gaze was fastened on her as they chatted. As they approached a driveway, he paused, looked both ways, and then put his hand to the small of her back. Very protective, very chivalrous, very Tom. Sadie hoped this woman appreciated that.

Just as they drew opposite, Tom looked up. Their gazes caught. Sadie held up a hand in greeting. He nodded once and turned his attention back to his companion. Sadie breathed out, her shoulders relaxing.

Her life was beginning to feel very full with Jake in it, but she still regretted losing Tom's friendship. He was a good guy, and she hoped with everything she had that he got his happy ending.

She bit her lip. Was it too much to hope that she'd get one, too?

She waited only another couple of minutes before Jake arrived. He kissed her on the cheek, flashed his boyish grin, and said, "Hi."

One little kiss, one amazing smile, and one simple word and her heart did a happy flip. Dang. The talking-to she'd given herself this morning about trying to enjoy it without putting her silly heart at risk had been a waste.

It was a 1:10 game, and the sun was bright. They'd both peeled off their outer layers by the time they arrived at PNC Park. Jake wore a snug black Pirates t-shirt. He was tall and lean, but that didn't mean he was a string bean. His shoulders were broad, his tummy flat under low-slung jeans, his chest and arms plenty defined.

He caught her ogling him. "Like it?" He smiled and his brown eyes twinkled, but he waved a hand at the t-shirt. "I needed some new 'burgh gear. It's from that shop closest to the diner on Penn Avenue."

Sadie breathed a sigh of relief. He had to have realized she was drooling over him like The Wanderlust customers did over the dessert case, but he wasn't going to comment.

"I got you something recently, too," he said.

"Well," Sadie said, "what is it?"

"Patience. I'll give it to you next shift."

"That's hardly fair," she said. "You shouldn't mention a gift to somebody unless you are prepared to hand it over."

"Too bad," he said, but he looked inordinately pleased with himself.

Hmmph, she thought, wondering what in the world he could have gotten her.

They navigated security at the stadium and then stopped at a food counter. "My treat," he said, and ordered waters, a hot pretzel, and popcorn. "Want anything else? Pop? Beer?"

She specified a pop, and he ordered a big one.

"We can share," he told her, and casually put one hand on her lower back.

Amazing. The man could even make ordering from a concession stand sexy.

"You don't have to pay all the time," Sadie told him as they headed for their seats, because he'd insisted on treating Friday night as well.

"I want to," Jake said, and motioned her ahead of him up the stairs.

Sadie mentally shook her head as she climbed, hands full of snacks.

He'd buttered her up all week at the diner with all that flirting and teasing. The band outing had been a get-comfortable type of excursion—at least until they'd plastered themselves together while dancing. But this—casual as a ball game was—was an actual date.

Jake, it seemed, had begun formally courting her.

9

M onday night was generally a slow one for restaurants even in the popular Strip, so both Sadie and Jake had the evening off. He asked her to dinner under the guise of trying one of the newer restaurants downtown. When he was young, the city used to empty out after the workday, and he didn't recall anyone actually living downtown. People might come back for a show at the Benedum Center or a symphony at Heinz Hall, and, of course, any of the sports venues drew a big crowd. But the city had really come into its own in the last decade or so. These days there were restaurants everywhere downtown, and the unique periphery areas like the Strip District, the South Side, and Lawrenceville were really booming.

He figured two birds with one stone: start courting Sadie in earnest and get reacquainted with this new version of his hometown. He was also hoping it'd be a real treat for Sadie. He figured that between working all the time and paying her own way, Sadie probably rarely did anything expensive or fancy.

So, he'd told her to dress up, and he'd made a stop for flowers. As he rang her bell, he shifted his shoulders under his sports jacket. He hadn't anticipated being nervous and was glad he hadn't opted for a tie; he'd likely feel like he couldn't breathe. The car service he'd hired waited behind him, and Jake suddenly wished he hadn't brought along a witness to his first official date with Sadie. He wasn't sure if he should be counting the ball game or not.

He heard footsteps and looked up just as the door swung open.

Sadie was pure, gorgeous sunshine in a yellow printed dress and cropped pink jacket. It was a retro look, and yet on her looked as fresh and hip as could be. She smiled nervously, and he realized she was wearing a little more makeup than usual. Maybe lipstick instead of gloss? He didn't really care—to him, she was just as beautiful wearing a diner t-shirt and food slop.

"Hi," he said. "You look beautiful."

He leaned in to kiss her on the cheek. Because he'd decided to kiss her as often as possible. It was appropriate if they were dating or courting, or whatever they were calling it. And she'd need to get used to it if people were going to buy them getting married. They had to start somewhere. Soon, he hoped, maybe by the end of the night, he'd get a signal that she was ready to be kissed on the lips…

Jake pulled the flowers out from behind his back. "For you."

Her smile widened and she reached for them. "Thank you. I love flowers."

He hadn't known that and realized there was likely a lot he didn't know.

"I should put these in water before we go." She smiled shyly—so unlike Sadie to be so tentative. "Want to come up for a minute?"

Jake motioned to the driver that they'd be five minutes and followed her into the building and up to the top floor.

Typical for row houses like the Mexican War Street neighborhood, especially those that had been split into apartments, the stairwell ran along one side of the structure, and her space appeared to be railroad-style. The entry opened into the living room, and he had time to look around as she slipped into the kitchen at the right. He could see beyond the pass-through as she found a vase and grabbed some scissors.

The living room had a red futon, a printed chair, and bright yellow pillows. A series of prints of flowers—big, bold, and modern—lined the back wall.

He smiled. She *did* like flowers.

Her place was decorated somewhere between thrift shop and store-bought. Modern and spunky, but simple. Like the IKEA catalogue, where he'd chosen a lot of his New York stuff when he had to fill the place in a hurry. A laptop with stickers all over it, an open spiral notebook, and a soft-backed textbook had been set aside on the couch, and her backpack was on the coffee table. She must have been studying before he arrived.

A big bookshelf dominated the side wall and was filled with books and binders, random piles of notebooks and papers, and a few knickknacks. No TV, unless it was in the bedroom.

Jake corralled his thoughts away from considering the bedroom at all.

The car ride was short, and the driver stopped in front

of the Fairmount Pittsburgh. Dinner was on the second floor of the hotel at a new hot spot called fl.2. Weird name, but that hadn't stopped anyone. It was jammed despite it being a Monday. Thankfully, he'd called ahead for a reservation. Bonus: they were seated far from the circular bar, where it was a little quieter. He wanted to be able to converse with Sadie.

Once they were settled with drink menus, they discussed the pros and cons of the non-alcoholic "mocktails" that the trendy restaurant offered.

"Do you enjoy wine?" he asked.

She nodded. "I prefer red."

He chose a nice Argentinian Malbec, as he thought it fit the overall menu, they decided what to order, and once the wine had been poured, Jake raised his glass to Sadie's.

"To getting to know each other."

She sipped and then replied, "We've known each other for years."

"I knew fifteen- to eighteen-year-old you," he said, and chuckled when she grimaced, "but I'm only just discovering adult you. I know you have an amazing work ethic and that you still ride a bike to commute and have an adorable habit of ending up with three pens stuck above your ears because you are the fastest server in the east."

"Yikes." She laughed.

"But," he said, "I don't know what you're studying, I haven't asked about your parents, I'm wondering how you keep up with the Pirates without a TV in the living room, and I'm curious about what you plan to do when you graduate."

Sadie said, "That's an awful lot to cover over one meal."

He looked her right in the eyes. He'd always liked those big, warm brown eyes. "Don't worry. We've got a lot of meals to look forward to."

———

Sadie felt a little thrill at that idea. Months of talking with Jake? Sharing meals and ball games and outings? Texting him and flirting with him? Dancing with him and surely even kissing him? Maybe even getting seriously intimate with him?

Sharing an appetizer like they were now? Jake had even fed her the last bite, and all she could think was that she should take his finger into her mouth.

Yowza. And a good thing, too, because after her little panic yesterday, she'd given herself a smack upside the head and decided that, if nothing else, she should just enjoy this time with him. The worst that could happen (her heart scattered in little shards all over the diner's kitchen floor where everyone could see it and grind it into dust as they tromped back and forth) was probably happening either way. So, she might as well enjoy now and have it to remember.

Sadie took a deep breath, let the smile in her heart show on her face, and opened her mouth to share her life and let him in.

She told him that she was originally an elementary ed major but ended up loving a marketing class enough to double major. She talked about her job at the Children's Museum doing programming.

"It combines the best of both worlds. It's exactly what I want to do, and I feel lucky to have already found it."

Sadie's smile wavered. To cover, she reached for her glass and sipped some wine. She hated to even think of leaving the museum to go teach, but she wouldn't be telling Jake about going abroad anyway. He'd be long gone by then, and at least for now she could pretend it wasn't happening.

"As for my parents, my mom is still local. I see her sometimes, but mostly she does her thing and I do mine."

"Is she still tending bar over on the Northside?"

"Yep. Anyele's a lifer. You can often find her there even when she's not on shift."

"Your dad?"

"He moved to Georgia, apparently."

"No contact, then?"

Sadie knew Rita had probably let slip—or maybe she herself had when she was younger—that her dad meant well but wasn't exactly stable. Honestly, it was easier to have him gone than to be constantly on the yo-yo string that dealing with him always entailed. It was why, Sadie thought, her mom had been so emotionally distant—a coping mechanism that, unfortunately, had extended to her young child. They'd made inroads the last few years, though, because in many ways Anyele had grown up, once she was out from under her husband.

"Haven't heard from him in years and don't expect to. Mom thinks he's living with a psychiatrist—which is surely exactly what he needs."

Jake gave a serious nod. "What about after graduation? What are your plans?"

Sadie waved her hand. "That's for another time. I'd rather talk baseball."

Jake laughed. "Of course you would. So how do you

watch with no TV?"

Their dinner arrived, and after they nibbled a bit, she said, "A lot of the games are played when I'm at work, so I either listen to the radio or keep an eye on the score via my phone." She paused and waited for him to look at her. "I do have a TV in my bedroom. Maybe we can watch one of the night games together."

To her gratification, Jake's voice was extra deep when he said, "I'd like that."

Jake insisted on trying a dessert. Sadie would have passed, but he seemed to want to pull out all the stops tonight. She had a couple of bites of a delicious cheese-cake with spring berries, then leaned back in her chair.

"Turnabout's fair play," she told Jake. "I want to know what happened in New York. Why you decided it was time to leave and come run the diner."

"There's not that much to tell. Mainly I just became disenchanted after a while."

Sadie prodded him, and Jake explained about not enjoying his job, not liking the caliber of people he worked with, even tiring of the city somewhat. "I just didn't know how or what to change to. Always in the past, I've had my next steps in mind—or at least a wish list. But when you're on the fast track in a career, it's hard to see outside of it."

"So," she said, "what prompted this epiphany to come home?"

He shook his head. "This crazy team-building event in some little town called True Springs." Jake told her about cliff jumping and one of his team pushing a guy named Reese off and laughing. "It wasn't just that, though. Nobody was interested in getting to know one another. Hell, if they'd have thought their phones would have survived the water, they never would have stopped working."

"Not fun."

"No, and it could have been. The town was kinda cool. It's all built up around—" Jake broke off and shook his head.

Sadie said, "What?"

"Eh," he said, "that's a story for some other time."

"Come on," Sadie said. The fact that he didn't want to tell her something made her even more interested.

But the server appeared and handed Jake the bill. Once he'd handed off his credit card, he continued the story. "On the way home from the event, my mom called about my dad. I knew then I was done. No way was I wasting time somewhere I didn't want to be. Life's way too short."

A shadow crossed over his face, as it often did when somebody mentioned his dad, so Sadie decided to lighten the mood. "And Diner Boy came home where the three murky rivers, the gray days, and the harsh accents stole his heart all over again. Immediately, he knew it was the 'burgh forevermore."

"Pretty much." Jake laughed and stood.

"And the diner," she said, continuing the game as he took her hand and helped her up. "He realized he couldn't live without skating on grease and sweating over a grill."

Jake's eyes twinkled. "You forgot the part about seeing a wisecracking girl he used to know who turned into a gorgeous woman, which sparked a crazy-good idea in his head."

"Now that's a Shrek-worthy fairytale." Sadie smiled.

"But all true," Jake said, and pressed a kiss to the back of her hand.

10

———————

S adie felt a little glowy all day Tuesday. Fine, glowy wasn't in the dictionary, but that was how she'd describe it: somewhere between warm and gooey, nicely satisfied and filled with anticipation. Last night's official fancy-pants date had ended with a super-yummy episode on her front steps.

One of Jake's sweet kisses had started on her cheek and travelled ever so deliciously. Because he'd intended that or because she'd turned into him giving him the all-clear, she didn't know. Probably both. When he reached her mouth, she'd sighed. His hand had come up to cup her neck, and his thumb caressed her jaw line near her ear. He kissed her ever so softly, bottom lip then corners, making her melt and ache for more.

She'd grabbed a fistful of his jacket and came up on her toes—and then both his hands were on her head, their tongues danced, and yowza, but she'd heated up fast.

Jake was the one who broke away. He rested his forehead on hers and whispered hoarsely, "I've *got* to buy a car."

She agreed. And not just because she didn't want some car-service driver watching her get kissed to within an inch of inviting Jake to her bed.

Unlike New York City, in Pittsburgh, most people needed a car. Of course, *she'd* chosen not to spend the money on one, but in her case that was reasonable. Her apartment, jobs, and campus were all within biking distance, and she lived alone, eliminating the need for superstores or trips to the suburbs for this or that. If her bike didn't cut it, there was public transportation, car services, or her friends. And Rita and Chuck—bless them—always sent someone to get her or dropped her back home themselves if the weather was abominable.

Sadie eyed Jake this evening as she went in and out of Wanderlust's kitchen. He gave her a grin or a wink or some kind of acknowledgement every time. But even when his smiles weren't specifically for her, she still got the sense he was happy to be here. As in here, following in his dad's footsteps, helping his mom, in this neighborhood…away from New York.

She had a hard time imagining that everybody in his company was as craptastic as he said, but certainly it seemed the excitement of the big city and high-intensity career had worn off. Still, she remembered what he'd been like as a teenager. Always busting to go. Almost vibrating with the need to go and do faster, more, something else, somewhere else… He moved fast serving tables or mopping up a mess, but became supersonic when he'd pound out the back door and take off to who-knew-where.

The novelty of being home would wear off. Sadie just knew it.

And then, when he'd left a big wake of hurt behind him, South Korea would feel like a relief. She'd stitch back together the pieces of her heart, expand her horizons, and create her own adventure.

Midway through the evening, she ended up between customers and stepped out back to take a break and get a little fresh air. That was one thing about working all the time—she missed a lot of the fabulous weather. Tonight was perfection and meant to be appreciated, even if it was only for a few minutes.

She leaned against a support beam and watched the comings and goings of people crisscrossing the Strip to go to dinner or run errands.

Jake came out, too. He'd lost the apron, but still wore his bandana. She loved the way he looked in it, like a pirate or biker without all the tattoos and jewelry. Strapping and sexy, ready for anything. His snug t-shirt only enhanced the look.

She doubted she looked as good with a couple of pens jammed in her hair above her ear and milkshake drips all over her t-shirt, but Jake didn't seem to notice.

He grabbed her hand and tugged her back toward him, alongside the wall next to the door.

He didn't waste time, just kissed her right on the lips. A long press, then he breathed in deeply. On his exhale, he said, "I've been dying to do that all day."

Sadie raised her arms and looped them behind his neck, pressing herself flush against him. "Then why'd you stop?"

Jake's eyes darkened and then he'd kissed the bejesus

out of her for a few minutes right there for all the outside world—and even Saint Stanislaus Church—to see.

When sense returned, she pulled away, sliding her hands from his neck to his chest. Such a perfect chest: hard muscles and a heartbeat that thumped as fast as hers.

"I better go in," she said.

"You'd better," he agreed. He'd been holding her hips. He squeezed once, then released her.

"You coming?" she said.

He gave her a rueful smile and glanced down to make his point. "I need a minute."

Holy moly, she'd made Jake Walker hard.

Thank God, because she was near to liquid heat herself.

She could only grin and wink before going inside.

When Sadie left that night and unlocked her bike, she discovered that Jake had needed time for more than getting himself together.

Rubber-banded to her bike seat was an envelope marked *Sades*.

She smiled and ripped it open. Inside was a printout of an online shopping item. It showed bike wheels with glowing LED lights that formed pictures like cartoon characters and superhero logos. The non-lit-up pictures showed four black bars attached to bike spokes.

Sadie peered at her bike. Sure enough, her back wheel sported those bars.

Scrawled on the side of the page was a note.

Yours is a Pirates P.

xx

Jake

OMG. It was the gift he'd mentioned. He'd custom-designed her a bike decoration.

Sadie banged back through the door and flew into the kitchen. Jake was coming back into the kitchen himself from the other end. Sadie crossed the room, note in hand, and launched herself at him.

"I love it!" she said. Jake caught her and spun her around once. As soon as he set her down, she gave him a big smack on the lips. "How do I turn it on? I want to see it!"

Jake laughed.

Rita came through the swinging doors. Jake's arms were still around her. Had Rita seen Sadie kiss him through the door's windows? Sadie felt a second of panic then squashed it. Sooner or later, Rita would catch on—if she hadn't already—which was what they were aiming for, right?

"What's going on?" Rita asked with a raised eyebrow.

Jake didn't react as if anything was out of the ordinary. "Come see," he said.

But Sadie was too excited. "Jake made custom lights for my bike!"

They all tromped outside, and Jake used the app he'd downloaded on his phone to turn the lights on. It was full dark, and the thing *glowed*. Sadie jumped up and down and clapped. Her whole back wheel shone bright gold, except for the black Pittsburgh Pirates-style P in the middle.

Rita said, "Now I can stop worrying. No driver can miss that."

She was right. Sadie had reflectors and a front lamp, but this was so much better.

"Bonus, you can show off your team spirit," Jake said. "We'll need to get you the app."

"Thank you," Sadie said. "I love it. It's the best gift ever."

She had to force herself not to jump right back into his arms and kiss him for all she was worth right in front of Rita.

The rest of the week was spent kissing and laughing. Even at work, Jake pressed his lips to Sadie's as many times as she'd let him catch her. She laughed when she managed to spin out of his grasp—even if it meant he untied her apron in the attempt. He loved to hear her laugh.

On Thursday evening, Benny was on the grill, which meant Jake was mostly on the move. Not only did he catch Sadie for a kiss, he managed to yank her into the storeroom, shut the door, and pull her body to his.

Then he really, thoroughly devoured her. His hands roamed from her back to her waist to her ribs and right up to the underside of her breasts. When she threw her head back and moaned, he put his mouth to her neck and fondled her breasts. She dug her hands in his hair and pushed his head down. The next thing he knew, he'd yanked down the V-neck of her t-shirt, popped one breast out of her bra, and latched his lips on to the most glorious, dark nipple.

"Yes," she said, and thrust her hips against him.

He wanted that too but couldn't get any purchase, so he

spun them and pushed her against the shelving, where he could match her movements.

"Maybe we should break out the Firefly for this reenactment," she said in a throaty whisper.

He chuckled. "I always think of you when I smell or taste cinnamon." He went for her mouth again. "I still taste it when I kiss you."

She moaned his name and slid one hand over his back. The other was on his ass.

Just then, the door opened with a bang and he heard a gasp.

Oh. Shit.

Jake straightened and turned, careful to entirely block Sadie with his body.

His mom held her hand over her mouth and her eyes were wide. Sadie wriggled behind him and then went still. It felt like she'd curled against his back. He prayed that she'd managed to get that perfect breast back into both her bra and t-shirt. He reached behind him with one hand, and Sadie grabbed it hard.

"Jacob Alastair Walker," Rita said with complete horror in her voice.

"Mom, it's not what you think—"

"You have *no idea* what I am thinking right now."

"Sadie and I are—"

"I'm leaving," Rita interrupted. "You close up. Then come *directly* home, and I'll tell you *exactly* what I'm thinking."

Jake nearly gulped. "Yes, ma'am."

"Sadie," Rita said, in only a slightly softer tone.

Sadie stepped out from behind him, though she kept a death grip on his hand. "Yes?"

"Don't stay to close up. Get yourself home pronto. You don't have much time before the rain starts."

Then she looked from one to the other of them, serious worry pulling at her features and a fiery look in her eye. She shook her head, spun on her heel, and banged out the door.

———

"Sit down," Rita told Jake when he entered her kitchen.

She hadn't changed her clothes, just sat with a cup of tea. The travel magazine next to it lay unopened.

Jake sat. She looked at him with steady eyes but didn't speak.

"Mom, I really like Sadie." Her mouth tightened, and he tried again. "As in really, *really* like her. We're dating."

"You are dating Sadie—and you didn't tell me? Don't you think that's rather important? A girl who is like my own daughter?"

"It just happened so fast," Jake said. "We hadn't put an official name to it yet."

She shook her head. "You are going to break that girl's heart."

Jake's temper flared. "I'm going to marry her!"

And in that moment, he knew it to be true—not because he'd proposed some practical agreement for some crazy plan. But because he wanted, with all his heart—holy shit—to marry Sadie.

His mom took a shaky breath and raised her chin. "You two have always had a special connection. And in many ways, there is nothing I would love more."

"But?" Jake asked, trying not to let the bitterness he felt at this moment be heard.

"You be very careful, Jacob Walker," she said.

He leaned back in his chair, feeling like an insolent teenager. "Why don't you think she's going to break my heart? Why is this on me?"

She breathed in deeply, her nostrils flaring, and stared him down. "Because you've made a practice of chasing the next best thing."

He rolled his eyes. "Every guy dates a bunch of girls until he finds the right one."

She snorted. "You've certainly done your share, but I was talking about places, experiences, jobs—whatever shiny next that's on the horizon."

That hurt, and Jake froze for a moment to process it. Being willing to take risks, move forward, and pursue opportunities was a good thing. He'd never been haphazard or impetuous or stupid about any of it. He was just sure about what he wanted—and decisive when it was time to act. Like now.

"This is what comes next. I'm marrying Sadie."

She pressed her lips together. "We'll see."

Then she got up and turned her back on him. She put her mug in the sink, crossed the kitchen, and headed for her bedroom.

Feeling defensive and unjustly attacked, Jake had to fight the urge to yell and bash things. Instead, he swore and squeezed his head in his hands, elbows on the table.

That wasn't how he'd imagined telling her. And that sure as hell wasn't the joyous reaction he'd hoped for.

What in the world did *we'll see* mean? Didn't she

believe him? Didn't she trust that he knew what he wanted? Or did her reservations lay elsewhere?

Maybe, he thought with a sinking weight pressing on his chest, she didn't think Sadie was the right choice for him. Or worse—that *he* wasn't right for Sadie.

11

Things with his mom were a little tense, but Jake tried hard not to let it bother him. Sadie arrived early for her shift on Friday evening and pulled him into the office.

"What'd Rita say last night?"

"Not much," he said. "She told me to be careful." He grinned. "She probably thinks you'll break my heart."

"Yeah, right." Sadie rolled her eyes. "Seriously, what was said?"

She had no idea of her power, Jake thought. No idea how much he liked her, how deep in he was getting. She could *easily* crush him.

"I told her we were dating. She told me to be careful." Jake sighed. "Maybe she's worried we'll ruin our friendship or make things uncomfortable at work. I don't know." Jake was starting to worry about the same, but doing his best not to think about it.

Sadie frowned, and Jake wanted to rub the little crease in her forehead with his thumb. Or better yet, kiss it away.

But there was more he needed to tell her, and he suspected she wouldn't like it.

"I told her I intended to marry you."

Her eyes flew open. "Oh my God. You didn't."

"I did."

Sadie stiffened and went pale. She took a step back, away from him. "What did she say?"

"Nothing, really. I don't think she believed me."

Sadie shut her eyes, and Jake realized she'd been terrified to hear his mom's reaction.

"Sades, it's fine," Jake said. He moved in and took her cold hands in his. "We're doing this."

"Jake, maybe—"

"She'll get used to us being together," Jake said. "The way it went down was just a shock. We weren't prepared to get caught like we did."

"I don't know," Sadie said. "This suddenly feels like a very bad idea."

"It's a good idea," Jake said. And it was. He still wanted to give his mom her freedom and the gift of travel. But more than that... "I don't want to stop. I like you, Sadie. A *lot*. I *want* to do this with you."

His mom had planted doubts in his head that held him back. There was more he could say, more he would say if this situation wasn't half concocted. But it must have been enough, because Sadie dropped her head to his chest.

"We'll go on more dates," he said, and smoothed his hands up and down her back. "We'll keep kissing." He pressed a kiss to the top of her head.

Sadie shuddered out a sigh. "Okay."

Jake felt better already. "We just won't ever enter the storeroom alone together."

"Definitely not." Sadie laughed. "We'll save the hot and heavy for *outside* The Wanderlust."

Jake felt immeasurably better. He liked that idea a lot.

———

Mid-evening, Sadie slid behind the counter, where Rita was refilling the coffee machine. Her customers seemed to be content for the moment, and given that this was Friday night, this might be her only chance. Sadie knew she had to say something to Rita herself if she was going to have any chance of feeling better about all this.

"Rita?" Sadie waited for Rita to look at her. "I'm really sorry about yesterday. It won't happen again."

Rita crossed her arms and leveled a look at Sadie. "Are you two thinking better of dating, then?"

Sadie cringed. "No. I meant we'll keep things appropriate—professional—at work."

Rita nodded but held Sadie's eyes. "It's awfully hard to give advice when I love both of you, but I'm worried about you. Jake is a good man, but…"

Rita was worrying about Jake's staying power. No different than Sadie's own concerns.

"I know, Rita." Sadie reached out and squeezed Rita's arm. "I know exactly who he is, how he operates, and exactly what I'm getting into." She took a deep breath. "I made this choice with my eyes wide open."

Rita blew out a breath and uncrossed her arms. "Okay, then," she said, and gave Sadie a quick, hard hug.

The relief was so great that Sadie's eyes welled up.

After that, despite a steadily darkening sky outside, Sadie walked more lightly through the rest of her shift.

Rita acted like Rita. Jake was flirty Jake again. Sadie still had the usual worries, but Rita's blessing made all the difference.

Sadie thought about what she'd told Rita. She *had* gone into this eyes wide open. She knew Jake would eventually leave. She expected to get her heart broken. But she'd purposefully dipped a toe into this because she wanted the chance to be with him. To experience what she'd fantasized about for so long. Whether it ended well or didn't, she wanted this experience and believed it would help her move forward.

Sadie knew she'd been holding back. She hadn't been sure, had needed time to acclimate to this new reality.

Okay, fine, she was scared.

But if you were going to do a thing, it made no sense to do it halfway. Now was the time to strip off her life vest—maybe her clothes, too—and jump in with two feet.

If nothing else, she'd seize life and love for a while. Really, fully experience it with all her heart, if only she was brave and bold enough.

A few minutes later, Sadie pushed into the kitchen with a ticket for a table of six and clipped it up. Jake was turned away from the grill, and she watched the play of his muscles under his dark t-shirt as he worked. When he turned around, his face was flushed with heat under that red bandana. His eyes lit with pleasure at discovering her standing so close.

"Hi," he said with a wide smile, even as he reached for the griddle press and then the spatula without missing a beat.

"Hi, yourself," she said.

Jake had suggested they get a drink together after

work, but the Pirates were playing in Chicago tonight. There'd been a very long rain delay, which meant it'd still be on TV after work.

Sadie leaned a hip against the counter, reached up, and slid one of the pens out from above her ear. She looked at Jake, scribbled on her pad, then ripped off the ticket and folded it in half. With her heart beating hard, she pushed away from the counter and came in alongside him. She tucked the note into his back pocket, then rose on tiptoes and gave him a quick kiss on the cheek.

He raised an eyebrow.

"Let me know what you think," she said.

She went back out front only a little nervous. *Surely* Jake would say yes.

12

———————

J ake had rushed to his mom's after work, taken a lighting-fast shower, used an app to set up a car service, and hightailed it over to Sadie's. They both had the early shift tomorrow, given that Saturday mornings were the busiest time of week in the Strip, with everybody visiting the meat market and fish market treating themselves to breakfast before or after. So either way tonight went, they'd be short on sleep.

Now, as he stood at her front door poised to ring the bell, he wondered how short. Because Sadie's note had read:

No drinks tonight. I don't want to miss the game. Join me in my bed instead?

Jake's heart had beat double time, even as blood rushed south before he checked himself. Did she really mean what he thought she meant? Or was he reading his own desires into it?

He'd be cool with just spending the time with Sadie

and actually watching the game, but surely she wouldn't have added the bed part if she didn't mean...

Through the window, he saw Sadie's feet tripping down the stairs, then her knees, then a loose printed skirt. He was about to find out.

She opened the door. Over the skirt she wore a light pink t-shirt and—no bra. Perky breasts with pert nipples under a very thin t-shirt totally snagged his attention. Whoa. He managed to suck in air and drag his eyes upward to discover she was beaming at him.

"Come on," Sadie said. "We're up two." She grabbed his hand and tugged him along behind her up the flight of steps. Her fresh scent, like soap and spring flowers, drifted back to him. She'd showered, too. But then, when you worked in the food service business, you usually did after work. The lack of a bra was—hopefully—a far better indicator of her intentions. Holy...

As soon as he entered the apartment, he could hear the sounds of baseball coming from the bedroom.

"Do you want a drink?" she asked.

"Whatever you're having is good." He followed her into the tiny kitchen and leaned back against the counter, as she opened the fridge and bent over in that pretty skirt. It wasn't short, but her gorgeous legs were on display. There was nothing he'd like more than to run his hands from her ankles past where that skirt ended. Preferably with his lips involved, too.

He had to fight to stay where he was. But he was very conscious of taking this—whichever way it went—at her pace.

She twisted off the top of an IPA and handed it to him.

She leaned into him then, forearms against his chest, and kissed him. He widened his stance and smoothed a hand from her lower back up to her neck.

"I'm glad you're here," she said.

"So am I," he replied.

The game ramped up in volume, and she grinned. "Come on."

In the bedroom, she climbed onto a queen-sized bed. He noted purple sheets, a white comforter with a black floral design, and two mismatched nightstands. He didn't notice anything else because Sadie was patting the space next to her, even though her eyes were on the game.

He rounded the other side and saw she'd set out a glass of water for him and an extra coaster. He toed off his shoes, propped himself against the pillows, and put an arm around her shoulders. She tucked in close to him, knees up, which made her skirt ride up.

Jake dragged his attention to the game. Bottom of the eighth. "Must have been some rain delay," he said.

"They actually had a second one in the fourth," she said. "From the clips, it was a deluge." She smoothed a hand over his chest and looked at him. "And it's a *really* boring game."

She shifted, pushing upward to kiss him, her breast pressing against him.

Jake slid his hand behind her neck, the other down to the curve of her waist.

She shifted onto her knees, then swung one leg wide to straddle him. Jake's body surged and tightened.

"It's *so* boring, I don't think we need to watch it," Sadie said. She sank down onto his lap, took his face in her hands, and kissed him.

And whoa—things got hot fast. Jake sucked Sadie's nipples through her t-shirt and then ripped it off. He'd seen her tattoo before around tank tops, but now he got to kiss it, pressing his lips to her chest and shoulder. His hands travelled her legs—just like he'd wanted to in the kitchen —and found something wispy and soft underneath.

He groaned, and she rose up to yank his shirt over his head, then kissed her way down his chest and went to work on the fly of his pants. He levered up, pushing her back, and lavished her with attention. Lips, collarbone, glorious breasts. Her belly and hips. Then he started at the bottom. Toes with pale pink polish, calves, sensitive backs of her knees, inner thighs.

He pushed Sadie's skirt up and found skimpy panties trimmed in lace—the same color as the t-shirt he'd stripped her out of. "So pretty in pink," he murmured as he kissed around the edges.

Jake barely noticed the sounds of the game. He was completely tuned in to Sadie's moans and sighs.

She writhed and then raised her hips, telling him clearly that she wanted more. Jake paused to shuck his pants and boxers. The announcers whooped, and Sadie glanced at the TV.

"Cubs just scored."

"Don't care," Jake said. A girl who liked some hanky-panky paired with sports? This was probably every guy's wet dream. Him? He wanted Sadie's attention all to himself. "Not even a little bit. Not when I'm about to score with *you*."

He grabbed her ankle and pulled her closer to him, then crawled over her on hands and knees.

She laughed. "Ooh. I trump baseball. I like that."

She reached for him, wrapping one hand around him, the other teasing him everywhere else. He groaned his pleasure, her touch affecting him like no one else's.

When she picked up the pace, he grabbed her hand and pressed it to his mouth—silently thanking her, but also making sure she knew that wasn't how he wanted this sequence to go.

He hooked a thumb in her panties. "Time to go."

She smiled. "Oh, definitely." And she wriggled out of her skirt, too.

Jake's breath caught. She was so incredibly gorgeous. Both fit and lush. So sexy. So perfect. He lay alongside her, kissing her, his hands roaming, hers doing the same, their bodies pressing, sliding, writhing. He couldn't get enough.

She hooked a leg over his hip and pressed against him in a demanding rhythm. He slid his fingers over her rear and between her legs. So wet, so warm, so responsive.

"Jake, please." She gasped. "I'm dying here."

"That makes two of us." He kissed her hard, then felt for the pants he'd purposely left on the bed and shook a condom out.

Her hands didn't stop roaming over him as he did what he needed to protect her.

When he levered himself up, she spread her legs and grasped his hips.

Still he waited until she tore her eyes from where they were about to join and looked up at him.

"You sure you don't want to save yourself for marriage, Sades?" He was teasing, yet serious. He knew she was experienced, but he felt deep in his soul that if they did this, there was no going back. He'd never want anyone but her.

She gave him a wide smile. "I'm marrying *you*, Diner Boy. So it's all good."

That was music to his ears. Jake slid home to what he knew would be the best season of his life.

13

That weekend, Sadie and Jake spent nearly every free moment together: getting to know one another and exploring each other—usually naked. And the two weeks following were pure bliss.

They went out late to see another band (this time not at his brother Jeremy's place), strolled through the Three Rivers Heritage Trail on the North Shore, took the Duquense Incline up to Mt. Washington, and had a romantic dinner overlooking the city (she'd always wanted to try the Monterey Bay Fish Grotto and experience its glass-enclosed dining room with its stellar views of her city). They also found time to cuddle on the couch and talk, and had lots and lots of world-rocking sex.

No matter whether they were at work or play, they laughed, teased, touched, and kissed. Her classwork suffered only a little. Thankfully, the worst of her papers and projects had been already well underway, and because she was normally short on time, she tended not to let herself get behind.

If Sadie could have frozen time, this would have been it. All she'd ever wanted—and even better than she would ever have dared to dream.

Right now, it didn't matter that this was a manufactured plan. It didn't *feel* fake. It felt glorious. It felt solidly, wonderfully real.

And Sadie willfully ignored the fact that the weeks were slipping by, that Jake would at some point pivot and change his mind.

She also mentally stomped on any thoughts of teaching abroad. She wasn't lying to him when he wouldn't be here to see her go, right?

Jake had purchased a car in a hurry, which had made spending time at her place easier. Almost as quickly, he also gave up hightailing it back to his mom's in the middle of the night.

There was no doubt that Rita knew what they were up to. She also knew he intended to marry her. And heck, they were both adults.

She'd cleared space in her drawers so that Jake didn't have to live out of a suitcase, she'd made room in the bathroom for his hair gel, and as for the bed—she didn't have to choose a side. She and Jake slept wrapped around each other.

One morning, when neither had to be anywhere early, she woke to the sound of Jake in the kitchen. Something smelled delicious. She padded out to the kitchen in bare feet and rounded the pass-through.

"I can't believe you feel like cooking on your morning off," she said, "but yum." She didn't have a griddle, but he had just flipped a giant pancake in her only skillet.

"Hey, get back in there," Jake said. "I wanted to bring you breakfast in bed."

She smiled. "That's sweet, but you don't have to."

"Yes, I do." He shook a can of whipped cream at her. "I have serious plans for this."

Instantly, she warmed. Jake was an extremely attentive lover. Tom had been, too, but Sadie pushed away the stab of guilt regarding Tom. She couldn't help it if her body responded to Jake like nobody else. Theirs was a wild chemistry that defied logic.

"Strawberries?" she asked.

"Those too." He hauled her into his side, popped an already cut piece of juicy berry into her mouth, then kissed her as the burst of flavor hit her taste buds.

"Mmm," she said. "Far be it from me to thwart serious plans." She squeezed his rear and threw an extra pop into her hips as she left. "Hurry, though. I'm ravenous."

After they'd enjoyed breakfast, thoroughly enjoyed each other, and recovered somewhat, Jake propped himself on an elbow.

"Let's do this," Jake said. He smoothed a thumb over her cheekbone and looked down at her. "Let's make it official."

Sadie's heart skipped a beat—she was simultaneously thrilled and crushed. She searched his eyes but saw nothing unusual.

When she didn't answer, he said, "It's time. Don't you think?"

"From courtship to marriage," she said. "Stage two of the grand plan?"

"Why not? It'd make me very happy to marry you, Sadie," he said.

She pulled in a deep breath but couldn't quite make herself smile. When she'd agreed to this plan, there'd been a part of her that had hoped—so flippin' deeply that she barely admitted it to herself—that he'd end up falling head over heels in love with her. That he'd discover that she was truly the one for him, and he wouldn't be able to deny that this—this physical magic that they had in bed and this deep connection they had outside of it—was something special.

"Nervous, Sades?"

He dipped his head and pressed a kiss on her lips. They'd had honey on the pancakes instead of syrup, and he still tasted of it.

"Don't be," he said. "We're already practically living together. Nothing will change except a piece of paper. You don't even have to take my name."

That was just it, she thought. She wanted his name. She wanted all of him.

But all she'd end up with was a piece of paper. One that would signify a lie to the government, a betrayal of Rita's trust, and, most of all, that Sadie was a stupid, naive fool.

———

As it turned out, they chose a wedding date only a week away. Jake wanted to be married before Mother's Day because he wanted to have everything aligned before he presented his gift—the grand travel package—to Rita. And it turned out that Pennsylvania allowed self-uniting marriages, which meant they'd filled out an application online, taken it to the Pittsburgh City-County Building to have it verified, and then only had to wait three days before marrying. They didn't even need an appointment with the judge. As long as they had two witnesses, they could marry anyplace they chose and mail in the bottom of the license with the signatures afterward.

So, they were right on schedule—and yet she didn't feel ready. She *was* nervous. She had misgivings and plenty of worry. Yet she had promised. She had agreed to this plan.

And that's what it was. Jake hadn't given her any indication that it was anything more or less. All the dates they'd been on were part of the courtship she'd asked for. The sex, he probably figured, was a giant bonus.

When they'd told Rita at The Wanderlust, she put her hands over her mouth, and her eyes welled with tears.

"I'm so happy for you," she said, and squeezed them both together in a three-way hug. "What wonderful news!" When she let go, she wiped her eyes. "So soon! There's so much to do!"

To her credit, she never once asked if they were rushing things. Maybe because Jake had blurted out his intentions when Rita had first caught them together. Or maybe it was because Jake had done such a stellar job of courting Sadie—so good, in fact, that Sadie was a goner— and therefore, Rita was also convinced.

Jake laughed. "We want to keep it simple, Mom. We only told you because we knew you'd want to be there."

"But you have to celebrate," Rita said. "We'll keep it low-key—just the most important people. Here. Right afterward. I'll plan everything—you don't even have to worry about it."

Except they did—because the guest list kept growing,

and Rita wanted their input on every dish and detail. Sadie had little choice but to push aside her concerns and roll with it, and to some degree, she was grateful that there wasn't any more time to stew over it.

Wednesday evening, Sadie and Jake had settled side by side on the couch after they arrived home from the diner. She intended to log at least a little time studying (fortified with a cup of tea and a piece of mixed berry pie she'd brought home), while Jake streamed a show with his earphones in so as not to distract her. He'd already showered, and now munched on a few sourdough pretzels and sipped on a beer. She'd smiled. The last couple of nights he'd dozed off before he'd drunk even half the beer.

When Sadie had finished proofing a three-page essay, she popped the last bite of perfect pie crust in her mouth and launched her email. Then, since she knew it'd take some time to load, she went to wash up some and change into her pajamas.

When she returned, she settled closer to Jake, and he lifted an arm, tucking her alongside him. She put her feet on the table and her computer on her lap.

But as soon as she focused on the screen, her whole world lurched.

An email—from the airline—front and center.

Upcoming itinerary. Gumi, South Korea.

Dear God, they'd sent her plane tickets.

A terrible sense of disaster flooded her, even as self-preservation kicked in. She tried not to move a muscle, except the one finger that worked feverishly over the trackpad. She clicked, clicked again, and then finally hit the right spot, and her mail window shrank, then disappeared. She jerked her head to look at Jake.

He shifted his eyes to her reluctantly, caught still in his show. But he frowned when he saw her face and reached up to pull out an earphone. "What's wrong?"

She shook her head, the movement jerky. "Nothing, I..." She sucked an overly big breath in. "For a second, I thought I missed the deadline on this assignment."

He kissed her on the forehead. "It's been crazy with the wedding stuff this week."

"Sorry," she said. "Go back to your show."

By sheer force of will, Sadie relaxed her muscles under Jake's arm, but her insides were totally twisted.

That was a near miss. She'd dug herself a hole, buried her head, and steadfastly refused to deal with reality. And if she opened her mouth now, it'd fill with sand and she'd choke.

Her eyes swam with tears of frustration, blurring the words of her assignment. Not that she was seeing them anyway. Sadie clenched her teeth. She was so angry at herself for not telling Jake about Gumi the minute he proposed this craziness, for selfishly trying to seize a period of happiness in a situation that was slated for termination, and for loving everything about this make-believe world they'd created.

Worst of all? Every single second she spent with Jake, she fell harder for him.

The wedding was just two days away. She knew she should tell him before then. And yet...

Did a fake wedding and pretend marriage require honesty?

Perhaps not, but dammit, her friendship with Jake did. She thought so highly of him and trusted him, and she thought he felt the same. This giant lie of omission would change everything, though. How could it not?

Tomorrow. She'd tell him tomorrow evening. The minute they left the diner. She wouldn't even wait until they got home. If it was a complete debacle, and he called everything off—

God, she could barely stand to think of it. Maybe, just maybe, he wouldn't freak out, and together, they could think of a workaround, to salvage the plan for Rita. That was probably the only scenario Sadie could envision that didn't ruin absolutely everything.

Of course, she didn't want to hurt Rita, but when it came down to it, she didn't want to lose Jake. Her heart didn't care one bit that this was all smoke and mirrors.

He felt so right here beside her. They got along great, they talked, they laughed, they teased. Their connection in the bedroom burned hot. The daily care he showed for her, and even the plans he kept making…

Just yesterday, he'd seen a print in a shop window in Shadyside. It was a huge floral thing. Modern and bright— just her style. Jake had taken the artist's card and snapped a picture of the artwork on his phone. He promised that he'd buy it for her as a late wedding gift as soon as he found a house and that they'd decorate a whole room around it.

Would he bother with those kinds of thoughtful offers if he was just biding time? He must care for her. The question was how much?

No wonder she felt so caught in this untenable situation. The lines were so blurred that they'd disappeared entirely.

Sadie scrolled down the page of her paper, still

pretending she was working, when really her mind churned right along with the sugar and caffeine that had soured in her stomach.

Jake had said that the wedding itself changed nothing. In some ways, that was true.

If she fessed up and—best case—they still married, then she would still have some time. Not the six months they'd agreed to past the wedding, but a good two and a half months before she left for Korea. Time in which he might yet fall madly in love with her, confess that he'd never leave, and beg her to marry him for real.

He might also—once his mom was well into her adventure—announce that he'd had enough of playing house and slaving over a grill and hightail it back to New York. Or knowing him, somewhere else entirely, like Los Angeles or Rome.

Sadie chewed on the inside of her cheek. He'd go. One way or another. Because what man wanted long term with a woman who'd been lying to him?

14

Because Jake had expressed interest in taking as much of the pressure off his mom as possible, on Thursday, he and Rita finally holed up in Wanderlust's office and spent a couple of hours discussing vendors, deliveries, staffing, payroll, and more. Some of the details had changed since Jake had left for college, and yet his parents had run the diner much as they always had. With enough hard work to build something they could be proud of, enough business acumen to be successful, and enough caring and generosity to instill loyalty in both their staff and customers.

It was also clear to Jake that his parents had shared a true partnership. Even when they divided tasks for the sake of expediency or preference, they'd still kept communication open and made decisions jointly.

More than once, Jake felt himself getting emotional. He was so lucky to have parents like these and so proud to be part of the legacy they'd built.

Shortly before he was due to take over in the kitchen,

Rita got them each a coffee and a jumbo chocolate chip cookie to split. "We earned it," she said.

Instead of scooting her chair alongside his again, however, she swiveled it to face him. She leveled her best mom look at him.

"What's up?" he asked.

"That's the very question I wanted to ask you."

"In regard to what?"

Leaning back in her chair, she crossed her legs and linked her hands together over her abdomen, settling in for an interrogation. Jake didn't even know what he was in trouble for yet, but old habits died hard and his pulse picked up.

She cocked her head. "What aren't you telling me?"

"What do you mean?"

She reached for her cup, sipped, set it down, and then studied him. Jake had an urge to squirm. She couldn't possibly know about the agreement with Sadie, and yet what else could there be?

"I know there's something you aren't telling me," she said.

He rolled his eyes. "Why would you think that?"

She raised her chin. "I don't think it, so much as know it. The same way I knew when any of you boys were up to no good growing up. I just know."

"Mom," Jake said with exasperation, "I'm working and I'm spending time with Sadie. There's no time for much else right now."

"Speaking of Sadie…" He turned up his hands when she didn't continue, and she shrugged a shoulder. "You two got awfully serious awfully fast."

"So what? We've known each other forever. And I

thought you were happy for us." Jake reached for his coffee for something to do with his hands. The guilt about lying to his mom ate at him. And yet he and Sadie had been having so much fun that it was easy to forget that the relationship was a strategic one agreed upon over a hot pretzel and sealed with a hug.

Rita huffed. "I am happy for you, but why the rush to get married?" Her eyes narrowed. "Is she pregnant?"

Jake took much too large a sip of the still-hot beverage, burning his tongue and nearly searing his windpipe. "Jesus, Mom, no."

They'd been careful. She'd had her period since they'd started sleeping together, but how many weeks ago was that now? Damn. Worry suddenly wormed its way into his gut.

She pursed her lips and swung a foot, still eyeing his every twitch like a hawk.

Jake set his mug down on the desk and exhaled hard. "What do you want to hear, Mom?" Hers was one of the only opinions he cared about. He didn't want to hear a negative, and yet he asked anyway. Because the wedding was tomorrow. "Do you still have doubts about my intentions? Do you still think I'm not good enough for her?"

"I never said that, Jake, and you know it."

But the worst part wasn't her suspicion, or even her doubt. It was that she made *him* question things. Was he doing wrong by Sadie? Did he just want her so damn bad that he'd put his own desires ahead of what was best for her? She'd agreed, of course, but what about in the end? What did she stand to lose? To be so young with an annulment or divorce under her belt? Would it cause a rift in her relationship with Rita?

Or would he be the one with all the scars?

He shook his head. "I'm one hundred percent committed to this wedding and to running the business." He threw an arm out to encompass the office. "The reason I haven't settled down before is because I wasn't ready. Now I'm ready. And Sadie's the right girl. She's my future and the right person to partner with me in the family business."

Rita's expression was sour.

He added, "I know you aren't going anywhere anytime soon, but it's still important that Sadie is nearly as wedded to this place as I am."

"That sounds like a business maneuver more than a marriage."

Damn it, Jake thought. She was too perceptive by half, and he was bungling it, too. Why had it come out of his mouth like that when he hadn't thought of the agreement in business terms for weeks?

"All I can tell you," Jake said, "is that I feel it in my gut that this is the right move. And my gut has never before steered me wrong."

"That's true enough, at least," Rita said.

He wasn't willing to say more now, when he hadn't even admitted to Sadie how he felt about her. Jake rubbed his forehead, then looked his mom square in the eye. "Do we still have your blessing?"

"Of course," Rita said. "Of course you do." She stood and opened her arms. He rose and hugged her. She gathered the coffee cups and left him the cookie. Neither of them had touched it.

When she reached the door, she said, "There better not be a grandbaby in my Christmas stocking, or you're in big trouble." Luckily, a wink and the hint of a smile accompanied her parting shot.

Jake huffed out a laugh. He suspected she'd like nothing more. Oddly, the idea didn't sound that bad to him either.

———

On Thursday, Sadie went straight from her day job at the Children's Museum to The Wanderlust for her evening shift. Jake was holed up in the office, Benny was on the grill, and Rita, who'd been out front taking care of customers along with Denise, asked Sadie to get several items from the storeroom.

As soon as she went in, she heard Jake's voice through the venting system. She smiled. Even from far away, through metal ducts, she liked his voice. Although she liked it best right up against her skin, when she could actually feel its deep rumble. She squeezed her eyes shut for a moment in a quick prayer that after she fessed up tonight, Jake would still want to be with her.

"Barcelona?" Jake said. "Reese, that's awesome, man. I've heard good things about that group."

It was quiet for a few moments, as Jake listened to whatever Reese was saying.

Sadie remembered that name from the story Jake had told about his team's visit to that little town called True Springs. She searched for the items she needed, shifting boxes as needed.

Jake's voice again: "That soon?" Another pause, and then he said, "Sure, toss my name in the ring. I'm not promising anything, but I'd be interested in hearing the details."

Sadie froze, one hand clutching a huge pack of napkins to her chest, the other deep in a box of coffee filters.

Not New York or Rome, then. *Barcelona.*

That was where he'd go as soon as he broke her heart. Well, wasn't that just craptastic.

With slow movements, Sadie set the napkins and filters on the shelf. Then she wrapped her arms around herself. Tears threatened, but she willed them away. She had known this was a possibility. Even Rita had known it— had, in fact, warned Sadie about it.

At least now, she could relax. She likely wouldn't have to tell Jake about South Korea at all. Because if the past was any indication, when Jake made a life change, it would happen fast. Full steam ahead, no time to waste.

She wanted to sink to the floor and nurse a good pity party, but she didn't. She forced herself to breathe deeply and pull it together.

Okay, then, she thought. She'd fulfill her promise. She'd pretend this wedding was her absolute dream come true. Easy enough, since it was. And until he actually left, she'd enjoy the hell out of all of it. Because it was highly unlikely she'd ever marry again.

In a cruel twist of fate, her heart would be Jake's forever.

15

———————

Jake wasn't normally a worrier. But he watched Sadie's mood rollercoaster up and down all week. Was she just nervous about the wedding? About lying to his mom or about actually marrying him?

Did she clue in somehow that he'd stopped thinking of this as a practical agreement? That he'd begun to feel he was meant to be with her, despite the way their being together had started out? Or was she feeling smothered under the wedding plans and all his attention? Maybe she was panicking that he wouldn't want to let her go, as he'd promised.

Jake should have opened his mouth and flat-out asked. But he wasn't sure he wanted to know the answer, and there never seemed to be a good time. Planning a wedding celebration in a week—even as low-key as they'd done it—made for a helluva busy week.

She seemed to enjoy spending time with him—just as much as he enjoyed spending time with her. But he often caught a shadow pass behind her eyes. He just couldn't decide what it meant. Regret? Sorrow? Unhappiness? Worry?

He'd just keep courting her, he figured, keep treating her nice—dinner dates and no-occasion flowers. More breakfasts in bed and more excursions in the city where they could hold hands and talk. Hot sex where he always, always put her needs before his own.

Maybe the six-month end date would pass, and she wouldn't even notice.

But if she did and she wanted out, he'd give her that, as promised. He knew now he'd never be able to be just friends with Sadie again—not really. Oh, he'd pretend— for her sake, for his mom's. But he couldn't imagine not always wanting her. Still, he'd do his best to ease his wrecked heart by being grateful that she'd blessed him with her time, her laughter, and her body at all.

Or hell, if he fell even harder between now and then? Maybe he'd just flat-out beg her to stay.

Thursday night, however, Jake's fears were alleviated. Sadie had seemed easier both at work and on the way home.

She showered first, covering her hair as she often did, and by the time he got out, she'd lit candles and donned a very sexy piece of lingerie—white and lacy and so stun-ning—and a silk robe. God, everything about her and everything she did just slayed him.

"It's my wedding-night outfit," she said, crooking her finger at him from the edge of the bed where she sat with her smooth legs crossed.

"So we get to enjoy it twice?" he asked, and dropped his towel to let her see just how much he appreciated the thought.

She smiled like a cat with her eye on some cream. "Maybe," she said. "Just in case we're too tired tomorrow night, I wanted to make sure you didn't miss out."

"Now that I've seen you in this, I'll be conserving my energy," Jake said. He took her head in his hands and started to kiss her, but she pulled away.

"Uh-uh-uh, Diner Boy. Hands off the hair. I want it perfect for tomorrow."

He blinked—he'd been so entranced by that gorgeous piece on her sexy body that he had forgotten. She'd spent hours at the salon getting fancy curls, even though she usually preferred more natural styles she could manage herself.

Jake pulled her up to standing and pushed the robe off her shoulders. "You'd better be on top."

———

The afternoon of the wedding, Jake drove, parked, and escorted Sadie and his mom to the bottom of the Duquesne Incline. Anyele, Sadie's mom, was waiting there already, and she beamed at them.

"Baby girl," she said, and opened her arms for a hug. "This is exciting."

Jake wasn't sure if Anyele was more excited about Sadie marrying or just so pleased Sadie had invited her to witness the event—not that it mattered. All he cared about at this moment was making Sadie happy, today and for as long as she'd let him.

To that end, when Sadie said she'd like to be married at one of Pittsburgh's most famous landmarks, he rolled with it. As it turned out, although the incline's cars were gorgeous and iconic, the approximately three-minute ride up Mount Washington didn't seem long enough even for the simplest of vows. Instead, they'd decided to incorporate the incline but actually exchange rings on the observation deck, which was more like a patio fenced in with red and black iron spikes, next to the museum at the top.

Rita was ready with the marriage certificate secured to a clipboard—just in case it was windy. And Anyele, who was quite a good photographer in her spare time, had been asked to capture the event.

To that end, once they'd bought tickets and boarded, she ushered them toward the front of the car and had them sit on the antique wooden bench under the front window. As always, Jake was shocked at how steep the ascent was. Sadie put her nose practically against the glass to look down, then grinned at him.

"It never gets old," she said.

"Neither does seeing you smile," he told her.

Her smile turned sweet and soft, and then Anyele said, "Snuggle up, you two."

Sadie slid over and nestled against him, and Jake brought her hand to his lips for a kiss. The other passengers stayed toward the rear of the car on the track side but watched avidly with smiles on their faces. If Sadie's beauty and his moonstruck grin didn't give them away, then the bouquet and boutonniere that Rita had insisted on did. Everyone loved a wedding.

"Now kiss," Anyele ordered them.

Sadie raised an eyebrow, but Rita said, "On the way back down. Let's get them married first."

In no time at all, they were standing on the observation deck. The day was ideal—mild and golden, perfectly showing off Pittsburgh's cityscape across the river. But Jake's eyes were fastened on his bride.

Sadie was absolutely stunning in a white dress with a bold pink, purple, and green swash of flowers that swirled from one breast to that hip. The dress fell just above her calves, and she wore pink heels, pink lipstick, and her hair curled into pretty loops. Jake felt like the luckiest man alive.

They waited patiently while a family finished taking photos, then stepped up to the wrought-iron rails.

Rita had taken Sadie's bouquet and then joined Anyele, who was already snapping away rapid fire.

Jake was cool with his brothers joining them at The Wanderlust to celebrate, but as he turned and took both of Sadie's hands in his, he would have given anything to have his dad here. He swallowed a lump in his throat. Chuck had always adored Sadie, and Jake expected he was grinning like mad from somewhere.

Rita dabbed her eyes with a tissue, and Jake was sure she was thinking of him, too.

He filled his lungs with air, and Sadie nodded.

"I know we decided not to write formal vows," he began, "but I just wanted to say that I became the luckiest man alive when you agreed to marry me. I promise, from this day forward, to honor and cherish you, to do everything in my power to put you first, and to do my best to make you happy always."

"Jake," Sadie said, "you are"—she drew a deep breath—"my very own dream come true." She opened her mouth, but her eyes welled with tears and she shook her head.

Jake smiled. He knew how she felt. It was incredible

and momentous—and totally overwhelming. He didn't see any shadows behind her eyes, nor did she seem nervous. But this was a *big* deal. *Far* bigger than he'd planned. There were hardly words.

Sadie pulled one hand from his and made a rolling motion—as in, *I can't speak, just get this show on the road.* He laughed, squeezed her other hand before letting go, and pulled the ring box out of his pocket.

He opened it. Two platinum bands: hers with an intricate floral design carved into it, and his had two grooved parallel lines.

He saw Anyele step closer and twist the lens of her camera for a close-up. As soon as she'd backed off, he took Sadie's ring out. She held out her bare hand. Bare only because Sadie had insisted she didn't want an engagement ring, but he'd secretly promised himself to make up for that later.

He held her eyes as he slipped it on her finger. "With this ring, I thee wed," he said.

Sadie squeezed his hand, then released it to take his ring from the box. He tucked the box back into his pocket, and then she was holding his left hand in both of hers.

"With this ring, I thee wed," she repeated. He felt her hands tremble before she slipped the ring on his finger and looked up at him.

They both broke out in wide smiles.

Sadie spread her arms wide, like *well, that's that, then.*

But she wasn't getting off so easy. Jake swooped in for a kiss, then scooped her up and spun her around. He felt so much joy in this perfect moment that his heart wanted to burst right out of his suit jacket.

Rita and Anyele clapped and whooped—and now, Jake

noticed, so did the small crowd that had gathered both within the fencing of the observation deck and just behind it on Grandview Avenue.

Sadie laughed and leaned into him, and he put his arm around her.

The moms doled out hugs and congratulations, before Rita pulled the clipboard out of her bag and said, "Let's make this officially official."

She handed Anyele a fancy pen, then took her turn. Anyele snapped a picture of the document with the two witness signatures—just in case, she said—and Rita tucked it away for safekeeping.

One of the onlookers offered to take photos of all of them together, and then they got some of each mom with her own child, then both moms with each.

They re-entered the building, but for once, no one took time to look at all the old pictures of Pittsburgh in its smog-filled days. Rita and Anyele gushed and trailed behind as the newly married couple went to wait near where the incline would arrive.

It was a tiny building, and Jake heard Rita say to Anyele, "I know we are celebrating a wedding, but it reminds me. We'd be honored to throw Sadie a little graduation party next month at the diner."

"That's so generous of you," Anyele said. "I'm sure Sadie would love that—if you're sure it isn't too much."

Sadie squeezed his hand. "Rita is so good to me," she said, emotion brimming in her eyes.

"She loves you," Jake said. He had the urge to open his mouth and say more, to tell her how he himself felt, but the moms were approaching.

In no time at all, the cable car hitched to a stop before

them, and somehow, they ended up riding down with just their party alone.

The moms, who'd both worn heels for the occasion, sank onto the gleaming bench along the rear. Jake went over to thank them both with a kiss and a hug.

Rita said, "May you and Sadie share as many good times and blessings as your dad and I did," and then burst into tears again.

The epiphany hit Jake like the car's cable had snapped clean through and barreled without restraint toward obliteration. No stopping the realization. He wanted *that*—what his parents had had. He'd been thinking he wanted to hold on to Sadie, but he hadn't been considering what that meant realistically. Forty years of marriage, with its ups and downs, joys and heartbreaks, a family—the whole shebang.

He was, he realized as they all tromped off the rail car at the bottom, in *deep* trouble.

He'd persuaded Sadie to go along with his practical charade as a means to an end. He'd offered a pretend relationship, for a limited time only. Hell, he'd even given them an expiration date. Six months from the wedding.

But he wanted more. So much more. He wanted it all.

He wanted to hang on with both hands and *never* let her go.

Long term. In sickness and in health. For better or worse. All of it.

Holy shit.

There was nothing for it, then. He would love her so damn hard that she'd have to love him back.

16

They'd closed The Wanderlust to patrons for the evening. Instead, it was jammed with family and friends, including Jake's brothers, aunts, uncles, and cousins; Sadie's mom, her friends from the Children's Museum and from Duquesne University; and some of the diner's regulars who'd become like family long ago.

Rita introduced them as Mr. and Mrs., and Jake and Sadie kissed—not too passionately—in front of nearly everyone important to them and then laughed along with all the cheering. After they'd thanked their guests for joining them to celebrate, Rita gave them blessings from her and Chuck, and then instructed everyone to help themselves to food and drink.

It didn't take long until silverware clinked on glassware, and a chant of "kiss, kiss, kiss" was taken up. Sadie looked only a little embarrassed, so this time Jake gave her the kind of kiss he'd been wanting to all afternoon.

He wanted to shout it from the rooftops: Sadie was his —at least for now—and he was the luckiest man alive.

Aunt Reenie squeezed their arms and squealed her congratulations. She'd managed to get Jake and Sadie alone enough to ask when he planned to tell his mom about the gift. "Next Sunday, for Mother's Day. And you ladies depart three weeks later."

"I hope that's enough time," Sadie said.

"I'm already preparing," Reenie said. "It's Rita you have to worry about it."

Jake said, "We'll help her get ready. There won't be anything for her to worry about here or at the house, because we'll be holding down the fort."

"It never fails." Reenie clasped her hands together and got weepy. "There's always some sort of unexpected good that comes out of a tragedy, and you two are it."

"I do wish Dad was here, though," Jake said.

"He's here, believe me," Reenie said.

Sadie had already introduced Jake to all her friends, and now tall, flame-haired Lilian came back over bearing her gift.

"Congrats again, you two," Lilian said, beaming. They chatted for a few minutes, during which—like everyone else—she asked about a honeymoon.

Jake had been kicking himself all night for not thinking about it sooner. They would have a hard time getting away for long with his mom due to leave and a business to run, but surely they could manage a weekend trip. They could always go somewhere more exotic later—if, of course, Sadie hadn't packed up at the six-month mark. He felt a roll of fear in his gut at the thought but pushed it aside.

"Speaking of," Lilian said, "you know how I am about gifts. I get so excited. Open it now." And she thrust the wrapped package at Sadie.

"If we must," Sadie said with a grin. She tore open the package, froze for a second, then clasped it to her chest.

Jake was confused. "*Korean for Dummies?*"

"I've always wanted to learn," Sadie said, then turned to Lilian. "Thank you. Jake loves to travel, too. That's so sweet!" She grabbed Lilian's arm and steered her away. "Let's get you a drink."

Jake frowned. That was a little odd and yet another thing about Sadie he hadn't known. Maybe—if they made it far enough to enjoy a lengthy exotic honeymoon—he should consider Korea.

His brothers crowded him then, and all thoughts of travel vanished. Both Walker boys resembled Jake in terms of build, but Jeremy had a harder look due to his intense nature, and Jonah forever wore an easy smile.

"Dude," Jonah said, "I didn't see this coming, but it's awesome." He half hugged Jake, and they clapped each other on the back.

"Thanks, man," Jake said, and couldn't help the wide smile that split his face. "I couldn't be happier."

Jeremy also did the one-arm-hug and back-slap routine. "Congrats, bro," he said. "Talk about a whirlwind romance. You sure didn't waste any time."

He raised his glass, and Jonah and Jake did the same.

After they drank, Jake said, "I know it seems crazy, but somehow it's not."

Jonah said, "Well, you've known Sadie forever, so that shaves off some serious time."

"That and maybe there was a little help from some magical spring water." Jake chuckled and shook his head, surprised the words had come out of his mouth. He'd barely thought about that silly legend. He hadn't even mentioned it to Sadie—well, especially not to Sadie.

"What?" Jonah asked with a confused look.

But Jeremy's expression was fiercer than usual. "Let me guess. True Springs."

Jake reared back in surprise. "You've been?"

"Yeah. Apparently even magic doesn't work on me." Jeremy laughed, but it was brittle. "I'm the exception to the rule. A True Springs reject." Jake opened his mouth, but Jeremy added, "Not talking about it."

"Whatever," Jonah said, and rolled his eyes. But Jake resolved to check in on his older brother soon to see what in the world had happened.

An older couple that had been frequenting the diner since the Walker brothers were young boys sidled up to them. Jonah greeted them, but Jeremy shifted to Jake's other side and clasped his shoulder.

"Happy for you, man," Jeremy said. "And we're all glad you're home. I always figured someday you'd get hitched to a perfect woman, but sure as hell never expected you back here."

"Neither did I," Jake admitted. "But it feels right. I wouldn't want to be anywhere else."

Jeremy excused himself to go lick whatever wounds he had, or maybe to slip out and head back to Vine, but Jake's mind returned to his own last statement. It was shocking, really, but he *was* content here. He thought about the trading job in Barcelona that Reese had recently called about. He planned to listen when Reese called again—he believed in never shutting the door on an opportunity—but honestly? He couldn't imagine taking it. Not even if Sadie would agree to go and live abroad with him.

He preferred to stay here at the diner and in Pittsburgh. He was home—right where he belonged. Jake looked around the restaurant, practically busting at the seams with family and friends—and Sadie. He was no longer trading air, as his dad had once said. He was trading in hot food and warm smiles and barks of laughter. His shares consisted of comfort, friendship, support, and community. And just maybe, the most valuable commodity of all —love.

17

———

S adie had marveled at how calmly she handled both the wedding and the celebration. She supposed learning that Jake would end up ditching his plans to take a job in Barcelona had made it all easier.

Was she going to be crushed when he left? Of course. Her stupid, stubborn heart loved him. But she was going to enjoy temporary Jake and fake marriage while she could.

To that end, she did wear the wedding lingerie again Friday night after the festivities—at least until Jake tore it off her. And this time, she wasn't concerned about her hair.

They slept in Saturday, spending the day together because Rita insisted neither of them come in to work, and then showed up for Sunday morning's chaos at The Wanderlust.

Jake took a break midday to attend a few open houses. He'd been debating between buying in the Strip or in Lawrenceville (so trendy and popular that it was widely referred to as "the new Brooklyn") just up the river and practically right next door. Both would still feel like city living. Either, he said, would keep them close to the diner and Sadie close to the museum, too.

When he returned, Sadie and Rita were both in the kitchen taking a short breather, since they'd been on their feet and hustling most of the day. Rita drank iced tea, and Sadie had been hungry and hot enough to go for a milkshake.

Jake's eyes gleamed. "I found it, Sades."

"Found what?" And then she remembered where he'd been—house hunting.

He ducked into the office and came back with his laptop open and balanced on one hand. "I found"—he worked the trackpad—"the perfect place for us."

Us, he'd said and seemed to mean it. Sadie thrilled at the word and simultaneously reminded herself not to get too caught up.

He glanced up with a mischievous grin. "Just think, if we live in Lawrenceville, it'll be like rubbing elbows with the Great One."

"You really know how to sell a girl," Sadie said. She adored the late Roberto Clemente—one of the best Major League players ever and a Pittsburgh Pirate for the whole of his career—and Lawrenceville was home to the Clemente Museum. "I don't even need to see the house."

She warmed that Jake knew her so well, but to a degree, she was serious. She didn't need to see the house, because she wouldn't really be living there, would she?

Jake dipped his head back toward the computer. "Three-bedroom townhome with a quaint backyard, modern amenities, walking distance to pretty much everything. I saw it earlier and it's perfect. It even has a one-car garage—that means one in the driveway." Jake's eyes sparkled. "Someday you'll want more than your bike."

"Let's see," Rita said.

He set the laptop on the counter and turned it for them. Sadie made herself look for a minute but couldn't focus on the details. She grabbed her milkshake glass and took it to the sink.

Rita's eyebrows shot up. "You can afford that? Without getting in over your head?"

"I can. And the realtor in New York says there's two competing bids on my apartment, so the timing is good," Jake said. "I have to choose one this afternoon."

Sadie busied herself flipping through her open tickets, but heard him ask, "Can you manage, Mom, if Sadie and I cut out a little early so I can show her before I make an offer?"

"Of course."

Sadie felt her chest constrict. He still hadn't mentioned the Barcelona job. Would he really buy the house if he was planning on heading to Spain? Maybe he just figured no big deal because he could rent it out. Or maybe the job offer had somehow fallen through. Maybe he was staying.

Could they feasibly end up in this house together? As in actually married and living together? She had trouble taking in enough air. Because he didn't seem like he was just pretending. He acted like this was going to be their house—together and forever, amen. Did he expect her to give up her apartment? Because...

Sadie looked at Jake showing his mom the listing, and suddenly she felt unsteady. She grabbed hold of the counter like an anchor.

What they hadn't talked about or planned ahead of

time was what they were going to do *after*. After Rita went off to travel the world…after they no longer had to pretend…after the six months of marriage she'd promised.

Sadie bolted from the kitchen, saying over her shoulder, "I have customers."

Mostly, though, she had to find some room to breathe before she spun herself into a full-blown panic attack. She beelined for the coffee machine, turning her back to the diners. There was already a full pot of decaf and regular. So, she stacked mugs—restacked them, really—for a few minutes until she had calmed. Then she took a big breath, told herself everything would be fine, and went to check on her tables.

Later, Sadie oohed and ahed during the tour of the house in Lawrenceville. Jake had even picked out a wall to hang the floral gallery print he intended to buy her. She agreed it was perfect, but her heart felt like it was splitting bit by bit—much like tearing out a seam. Every new room, every fake smile, and she felt another thread pop.

By the time they'd capped off Sunday night with a movie in bed, Sadie was truly exhausted, body and soul. She kept dozing and finally just gave in. She awoke later to Jake turning off the lights. He pulled her against him spoon-style, then tucked the covers in around her front. It was so sweet—and so gutting—that a secret teardrop slid down her cheek.

The next morning, Jake announced that he had a phone interview.

"It won't take long," he said as he settled on the couch with his phone, a pen and a pad of paper. His laptop was already open on the coffee table. "I'm just humoring them."

Sadie doubted that. Jake was going to get caught up, like he always did, by something new. She knew it like she knew when a customer was going to stiff her and decided there was no reason to listen in. She went off to take a quick shower, then dress. She didn't bother with makeup. She suspected she'd end up in tears at some point anyway.

As she headed for the coffee pot, she caught the tail end of Jake's conversation.

"Thanks, Rich. I appreciate the opportunity." Then, "Will do. You too."

Jake leaned back in the chair and stretched. "Well, that's done," he said. "It wasn't so much of an interview as an offer."

How could he be so nonchalant? Sadie felt almost numb as she sloshed coffee into a mug—and yet she realized she couldn't go on like this anymore. Cautiously, she sat down in the armchair, set her cup of joe on a coaster, and braced her hands on her thighs. Anger stirred, and she was glad for it. She was tired as hell of being a sad sack in secret, sick to death of waiting for a shoe to drop.

"When do you start?" she asked.

Jake cocked his head. "Start what?"

She huffed out a breath of exasperation. "The job in Barcelona."

He reared back. "You think I just accepted a job halfway across the world?"

She blinked, thrown. "What else am I supposed to think?"

His posture had gone rigid despite the fact that he still sat far back on the couch. "I didn't accept it," he said. "I wouldn't do that."

She opened her mouth but didn't find any words.

Jake scooted forward until his knees nearly touched hers. "Why did you think that?"

She gulped hard. "It's a very you thing to do."

He flinched, and Sadie could tell she'd hurt him.

"I'm staying," he said slowly and deliberately, like it was the only way to get it through her thick skull. "I told you that from the beginning."

Jake got up and left the room. Sadie sat struggling to shift her mindset around this news. It was the opposite of what she had expected. She'd been dead wrong. This was what she had wished—and yet feared.

Jake came out of the bedroom in running clothes and said he was going out. The snick of the shutting door might as well have been a bang for all that it made her shrink.

Sadie stewed for quite a while, and then finally forced herself to study for her last finals. No matter what else happened, she had to finish school—with good scores— and get her degree.

Later that afternoon, as if to prove he'd meant what he'd said about staying, Jake called the realtor and put in an offer on the Lawrenceville house. He didn't say much —but Sadie could tell that he wasn't quite as excited as he'd been. Her lack of faith in him had cut deep.

They walked over to Nicky's Thai Kitchen on Western Avenue for dinner. Normally one of her favorites, tonight everything tasted flat—much like her mood. Once they'd returned home for the evening, Jake read through the paperwork from the realtor and had a conversation with both the attorney he'd used in New York and one his mom had recommended that was better versed in local real estate.

Sadie put her head in her books once more, although her concentration was for crap. She found herself snapping the lid of a highlighter on and off, on and off, and forced herself to put it aside. She read the same page of notes twice and didn't register a word. Then she shoved a pen in her hair, only to realize there were three there already. She sighed. At least she hadn't dragged out the Oreos. She stole another glance at Jake.

For an afternoon off and evening spent together, it kinda sucked. They got along. They weren't fighting or silent. It wasn't quite what Sadie would call tense, or even awkward, but she didn't feel right or easy. And Jake didn't seem himself either. Basically, it was the first time that they hadn't been in sync—and she didn't care for it one bit.

Jake eventually turned on the TV in the bedroom, and Sadie joined him, snuggling up under his arm. When the show ended, Sadie turned to him and kissed his ear, his neck, his jaw, his lips, sorrowfully and sweetly. A gentle apology that she hoped would ease the hurt she'd caused, but that they both bore. Jake turned to her, and they made slow, tender love.

Sadie did her best to turn off her anxious mind and worried heart, and just feel.

18

———

By Wednesday, Sadie felt she and Jake were on solid footing again. He was as attentive as ever, while she tried to give as good as she got, and somehow the strain from the weekend eased away. She managed to largely sidestep her worry with the routine of a regular week—at least if she could keep from looking at the beautiful wedding band on her finger.

Midday, Jake got word that his offer on the Lawrenceville house had been accepted. So, at the beginning of their shift at The Wanderlust, they mixed up a flourless chocolate cake, licking batter off each other's fingers. After closing, they shared it with the rest of the staff in a mini-celebration. Regardless of their murky future, Sadie was happy for him, and made sure she showed it with a big grin and a special toast.

For his ears only, she whispered, "We'll christen it the first chance we get."

"I'm holding you to that." Jake winked, then kissed the spot on her neck that always made her squirm.

In only a few days, they'd be celebrating Mother's Day. Sadie recalled that Chuck had always made a big deal of it, insisting on a fancy restaurant for dinner, where Rita could try something new and be served rather than serving. He'd always let the rest of the non-Mom staff run the show at The Wanderlust, and he and the boys had taken Rita to Mount Washington or downtown, or even a gem he'd heard about in the suburbs.

Rita insisted that this year she just wanted Jake to cook something light and have an impromptu meal late afternoon or early evening at the diner.

"It's time to make some new traditions," she said.

Sadie knew Rita just wanted to keep busy and not dwell on the fact that it was the first holiday without Chuck. She also knew that Mother's Day meant the diner would be really slow Sunday evening, but that they'd have a jam-packed morning—right up until about two o'clock.

Sure enough, that was how it ended up. When the place emptied out, Jake called his brothers and grilled some chicken to add to a Greek salad, and Sadie plated the pastries she and Jake had gotten from Rita's favorite Italian market down the street.

Jonah showed up with flowers and a kiss for his mom, and Jeremy with a card that he told her she couldn't open until later.

Jake looked around the small group. "Gifts first? Then we eat."

Assent all around. Except for Rita, who narrowed her eyes. "What have you kids cooked up?"

Sadie smiled. The woman knew when her boys were up to something, that was for sure.

Jake handed her a gift bag, and Rita set it on one of the

tables. She pulled tissue out of the top, then a glossy folder. Sadie knew it held an itinerary and numerous brochures and a printout of the first set of plane tickets. Others were yet to be purchased depending on Rita's preferences.

Rita scanned the items trying to make sense of it all, then looked up, eyes wide. "What in the world?"

They all laughed.

"That's exactly it, Mom," Jake said. "We wanted to give you the world. All—or most, anyway—of the places you've always talked about going."

Rita put her hand over her chest. "That's so thoughtful. Amazing. But…"

Sadie, of all people, knew how scary leaving home could feel. She said, "Reenie is going with you."

"And Sadie and I will be here taking care of The Wanderlust," Jake said. "Even Jonah has agreed to pitch in if we need him."

That drew a laugh from everyone, as Jonah really was near to hopeless when it came to the diner.

"Here, Mom," Jeremy said. She opened his card and found a gift certificate to a travel store. "I thought you could use some new luggage."

Sadie gifted her with a passport wallet that hung around her neck and could be tucked under a shirt or jacket for safety. And Jonah pulled a gift card—no wrapping—from his back pocket. "For travel books."

"This is all too much," Rita said.

"It's not, Mom," Jake assured her. "Like you said, it's time for something new."

Rita drew a deep breath, and Sadie could tell she was trying not to cry.

"Let's eat," Jake said, "and we'll tell you all the details."

———

Jake's excitement carried over, and he talked the whole car ride home about his mom's trip, the new house, and even his plans for some menu updates at the diner. Much as she loved her LED bike lights, once Jake had wheels, they usually drove, which was fine, because she enjoyed the extra time with him.

When they entered their apartment—she'd stopped thinking of it as *hers* weeks ago—Jake switched gears.

"I know we did the low-key wedding thing," he said, "but I was thinking we should honeymoon before my mom leaves. It'll have to be a quick trip for now. I was thinking about True Springs—that place I had the team event? It'd be very romantic for a couple."

Sadie stopped cold. Every day, practically every minute, Jake surprised her. It wasn't like she'd dated a bunch of rotten men—but somehow Jake had a knack for fulfilling every secret hope in her heart. A simple, romantic *honeymoon*.

He was busy depositing his keys on the counter and unloading some food that Rita had sent home with them into the fridge. He hadn't looked at her yet.

"Or you choose," Jake said, still facing away from her. "Where do you want to go? I like the guy who did my mom's package. We could just tell him where and let him handle the details."

Finally, he turned.

Sadie's eyes had welled with tears so fast that she couldn't hide it.

"Hey now," Jake said coming in close to rub his hands up and down her arms, "what's wrong?"

"Thank you," she managed. "I just didn't expect we'd go anywhere." She waved a hand. "Happy tears. Nothing's wrong."

Except it was. Terribly, horribly, awfully wrong.

She didn't want to go *anywhere*. Everything she wanted was right here—and so perfect that she wanted to weep with joy.

Which meant that everything was wrong. Because she would be leaving.

Not Jake. *Her*.

She pulled away from Jake. "I have to go shower. I stink."

Sometimes Jake joined her in the shower, or she him. This time, Sadie locked the door. Because right now, this minute? She needed to be alone. She needed to fill the tub to the rim with ugly tears and then stay under the water long enough to erase the evidence.

She blasted the water and stripped, leaving her clothes in a heap. Then she stepped under the showerhead, yanked the curtain closed, and sobbed her heart out. It wasn't a hairwashing night, and she'd completely forgotten her shower cap. She didn't even care.

Jake hadn't left.

He'd married her.

He'd bought them a home.

And worst of all? This evening she'd overheard a conversation between Jake and Rita that could only mean one thing. They'd spoken to the Walkers' attorney about making Jake half owner of The Wanderlust.

Only the other half wasn't to be Rita, but Sadie.

Her. Sadie. The same woman who had committed to two whole years on the other side of the world and still hadn't had the guts to tell Jake.

No two ways about it now. She *had* to tell him.

Tomorrow or bust.

Because the wedding was part of their deal. The house he could live in alone or—God help her—with some other woman eventually.

But The Wanderlust? No. Just no. She couldn't let him do it. It was Rita's and Chuck's. Jake's. Jeremy and Jonah's. But not Sadie's. Not with an enormous lie between them that would ruin any chance she had had at a real future with Jake.

Sadie clutched her stomach and then grabbed a towel and scrambled out of the shower. She made it to the toilet just in time. Then she cleaned her mouth, looked at her sad, sorry face in the mirror and sopping hair, and climbed back in the shower to cry some more. If only she could wash away her regrets.

19

———

Jake was waiting for Sadie to come home from the museum Thursday afternoon when the doorbell rang. He was thrown for a second—had she forgotten her key?

The building didn't have an intercom, so he jogged down the stairs to the first floor.

It wasn't Sadie, it was her friend Lilian. No mistaking that bright red hair. The stoop was narrow, so she moved back onto the stairs to make room for him.

"Hi," he said. "Sadie must be running late. She's not here."

"No worries," Lilian said. "I just came to drop off my backpack." She slid a big, but empty, pack off her shoulder and set it at his feet.

Sadie hadn't mentioned Lilian stopping by, and it was a serious backpack—for major hiking or camping or traveling the country. Jake cocked his head. "Are we storing it for you?"

Lilian laughed. "No, it's for her trip, so she doesn't have to buy one herself. The good ones don't come cheap."

Jake had a sinking feeling, but he asked despite a very strong urge not to know. "Which trip is this?"

"The one to Gumi, silly. She should have weekends off and be able to travel."

Jake swallowed hard. The backpack, the language book, the secrets behind her eyes—just what in the hell hadn't Sadie told him?

Just then, Sadie slid to a stop on the sidewalk below them. She straddled the bike and looked at them. Then, very slowly, she climbed off, propped the bike against the tree, removed her helmet, and hung it on the handlebars. She stared at Jake the whole while.

She stepped forward, arms stiff and hands fisted, like a toy soldier marching to its death.

Around clenched teeth, he asked, "When?"

She whispered, "Two months."

Lilian looked back and forth between them, her eyes as wide as bread plates.

"For how long?"

Sadie winced. "Two years."

Jake was so furious and so shocked that he thought he might actually explode—or maybe implode—on the spot.

He slammed the door behind him and stalked away from Sadie.

———

Sadie's stomach roiled like it fought curdled milk, and her whole body broke out in a sick sweat. Her heart actually physically hurt behind her rib cage, and she pressed a fist there. She wanted to disappear—or better yet, just die.

From the middle of the three short steps to the landing, Lilian asked, "You didn't tell him?"

"I'm sorry, so sorry."

But it was Jake that Sadie needed to tell. Just like that, her legs unfroze, and she bolted past Lilian and the forgotten backpack, into the building and up the flight of stairs. She burst in the door, chest heaving, and said again, "I'm sorry!"

"I can't believe you lied to me," he nearly yelled.

She opened her mouth, but he was faster.

"Not mentioning a huge, game-changing, all-important thing like *two years* out of the country? What the fuck, Sadie?" Jake said, his voice dripping with disgust. "You married me."

Sadie had never seen Jake so angry, nor heard him so loud. "But not really," Sadie insisted. "It's not *real*."

Jake flinched, and his skin went from flushed to drained of color in an instant. "It's real to me."

"Since when?" She could barely breathe, yet somehow words rushed past her lips. "You proposed fake. You didn't offer me real. You never said differently. I thought you were still pretending!"

Jake shook his head. "When were you going to tell me?"

"I didn't think I'd have to." She crossed her arms. "I thought you'd get cold feet."

He laughed—but it was a horrible, mean, ugly, not-Jake sound. "Cold feet for a fake marriage?"

Sadie lifted her chin. "It's not exactly your MO to stick around, Jake. The minute there's another exciting opportunity on the horizon, you're gone."

"Look who's talking," Jake said as he grabbed his keys. "*You're* the one who's bailing."

20

—————

For the first time in weeks, Sadie crawled into bed alone. She cried herself hoarse, then slept fitfully. When she woke Friday morning, she discovered she'd gotten her period. Great. Way to make her feel even worse—though she knew her extreme emotions weren't hormone related. They were pure heartbreak.

She dragged herself to the museum, but barely kept it together during the workday. She forced herself to eat a bit here and there for strength, but it didn't help her stomach upset. She couldn't focus to save her life. Didn't manage a lick of work. Her eyes were red, her face swollen, and tears still sprang forth every few minutes. In short, she was a disaster zone.

She'd tried to call Jake a few times. He must have seen—or heard and ignored—the missed calls. She didn't leave a message, though. Because what would she even say?

Come early evening, she still hadn't heard anything back.

Sadie rode her bike to the diner feeling like she was

pedaling toward doom. Even if Jake slept at his mom's or brother's or wherever again, he'd be on shift now. She had to face him, likely not in private.

She'd considered calling with some excuse, but not only had she made this new reality, she'd only ever called out when she'd been deathly ill. She never wanted to disappoint Rita. And she'd always felt strongly that she was a person who met her obligations. You didn't just no-show. You did what you committed to.

Like going to Gumi.

She slid off her bike on the verge of tears and with a huge lump clogging her throat. She glanced at the back door of The Wanderlust, and the sinking feeling worsened. This could be bad, really bad.

With slow movements, she locked up her bike. Her heart clenched when her eyes caught the little bars on her spokes that made the LED lights work. Jake's custom Pirates design.

He'd been so good to her, and she'd ruined everything.

Sadie's lip wobbled, and she drew a shaky breath before peeling off her light jacket. Then she forced herself through the back door—and immediately heard Jake's voice from the kitchen.

Her heart sank like cement all over again. He was here, to stay. And she was leaving. Because she was a misguided idiot with an overly strong sense of right and wrong.

But who was she wronging here? Everyone? The kids in Gumi? The program coordinator? Jake? Rita? Herself?

Good God, but she was in trouble.

Sadie put her jacket on the hook and her bag on the floor. She bowed her head and tried to work up the nerve to round the corner and go into the kitchen. Rita came into the back hallway before she'd managed it.

"Sadie," she said. "I didn't hear you come in."

Sadie looked up, but the minute she saw Rita, tears spilled down her face.

"Hey, hey, now," Rita said, and scooped Sadie into a hug. "What's wrong?"

"Everything."

"Come on outside with me," Rita said. She took Sadie's hand and pulled her toward the door.

Sadie felt she could breathe a bit deeper out here, but yikes, what in the world to tell Rita?

Rita had tried a bench out here long ago, but it attracted a lot of drunk club-goers and teen smokers at night, which in turn meant a bunch of litter, so she'd removed it. With nowhere to sit, Rita went straight for the edge, bent to sit on the cement, and dangled her legs over. Sadie joined her.

Rita put her hand on Sadie's knee and squeezed. "You can talk to me, you know, anytime."

Sadie opened her mouth. Closed it. Opened it again. "I'm in love with your son."

Rita smiled. "*That* I already know."

Sadie looked down the street at this section of town she loved, then back at Rita. "I think I nearly always have been."

"I suspected that, too," Rita said.

"But right before he came home, I finally made up my mind to make a change. I signed on to go to Gumi, South Korea, to teach English."

Rita's eyebrows rose.

"For two years."

Rita's eyes widened and she reared back a bit. "Oh. Wow."

Sadie nodded glumly. "I didn't know," she moaned. "I didn't expect…all this." She waved a hand toward the kitchen. "I didn't expect Jake. And it all felt like it wasn't real…like a dream. So I didn't tell him right away, and then I kept putting it off, and now…."

Sadie burst into tears. Yowza, she wasn't a crier normally, but she couldn't seem to help herself. She couldn't tell Rita about the lies and the pretending part, but it was such a relief to talk to someone.

Rita scooted closer and put her arm around Sadie.

"Oh, honey," Rita murmured.

"I've ruined everything. I wish I could just stay here with Jake. And with you. And at the Children's Museum. But I made this commitment, and I feel I have to honor it, and now I'm going to lose everything," Sadie said, then sobbed.

Rita made some soothing sounds but mostly just let her cry. Eventually, when Sadie had calmed slightly, Rita said, "Well, now I know why Jake's such a bear *and* why he's been sleeping at my house. Did you give notice at the museum?"

Sadie nodded. "Yes. I wanted to give them plenty of notice. I leave in two months—mid-July—because the program director in Gumi suggested I arrive early enough to transition with the current teacher. I went for it because I figured I could both get my bearings and travel some in August before the semester begins." She rushed on, needing to tell it all, needing perhaps to make it exist in reality. "They already sent my work visa and plane ticket and assigned me housing."

"I'm guessing the museum can't exactly hold your job for you for two years."

Sadie shook her head. "They'll have to hire someone. I know they'd hire me again if they could, but there may not be room for me by then."

"What if Jake went with you?"

Sadie bit her lip. "Once upon a time, he might have. But now, he wants this." She swept a hand toward the building. "He's done with big cities and travel." She smiled and nudged Rita with her elbow. "It's your turn, anyway."

"Let me ask you this, honey," Rita said. "What do you *want*?"

Tears swelled again.

Rita continued, "*Inside*. If nothing else mattered. If there was no right or wrong. No losing jobs or husbands or letting anyone down. Just speaking directly from your heart—if you could have anything, what would you want?"

Sadie didn't even hesitate. "I want to stay here. Right where I am. With Jake. Here at the diner and the museum both. I thought I had to go live life and *do* something, like everyone else, but really, *I* don't *want* to go *anywhere*." She took a deep, shaky breath. "But I'm not sure if Jake can forgive me. And I committed to this program. They paid for everything already, and—"

"Hang on there with the buts," Rita said. "First of all, anyone who knows you knows what kind of person you are. It's a point of pride with you to show up and give a thing your all. Heck, in all these years, I think you've only missed a handful of days of work. Second, it's a fact of life that things change. People accept jobs and then can't actually take them all the time. I promise you there is someone just waiting to take your spot. Somebody else who is just desperate for the chance. As for the money—well, think on what can be done about that. There are always ways."

Sadie felt a stirring of hope.

"And as for Jake"—Rita squeezed her shoulder—"forgiveness is essential to love and marriage. Part and parcel of any relationship worth keeping." Rita stopped, chewing on her lip.

Sadie sensed there was more, maybe a scolding or some words of disappointment. "You can say it."

"Well then, one last thing to consider," Rita said. "No matter how spur of the moment or rushed this wedding was, don't forget you committed to Jake, too."

Sadie's heart actually hurt again. For the lies, for Rita, for Jake, for herself… She wiped her face and tried to fill her chest and breathe. Rita couldn't know it hadn't been real. Except it felt like the real thing. And Jake had admitted the same—in anger, sure, but he had. Oh, what a hellish mess.

"Only you can make this decision, Sadie." Rita pulled her tighter against her in a sideways hug. "Know that I love you either way. You are one of mine, and that's not going to change. Okay?"

Sadie managed a smile and whispered, "Thank you for that. For everything."

"Now, I'm going to go in and get your stuff and send you home, or for a long bike ride, or whatever you need to do," Rita said. "You take the night to think and make a decision that feels right. Envision as clearly as you can what it'd be like to live that decision daily—and then sleep on it."

Rita made to get up, so Sadie jumped up and offered her a hand.

Rita hugged her hard, then pulled back to look her in the face. "If your decision still feels right in the morning, you'll have your answer. And then you can determine whatever actions might need to be taken."

"Okay," Sadie said, and nodded.

Rita rubbed Sadie's arms. "If it doesn't feel right, you make the opposite decision."

21

———

Jake had retreated to his mom's place after the big blow-up with Sadie. He couldn't lie in bed next to her when he was still so thoroughly pissed off. Even separated, though, he hadn't been able to turn his mind off and had slept like shit two nights in a row. Up way too early and facing down the empty hours, Jake felt like a caged animal. No out from his careening thoughts. No escape from anger and frustration. And certainly, planning for the new house wasn't going to distract him. There was little point.

Sadie was going to Gumi, South Korea. For two years.

Going. To. South Korea.

He had to keep repeating it to himself, knocking himself upside the head with the reality of it. She had lied to him and she was leaving.

For one moment, he considering calling that guy in Barcelona and accepting that job as a means of escape from his wrecked heart and crushing disappointment. Just as quickly, he discarded the idea. He didn't want that life.

He wanted this life. Not that it would ever feel right without Sadie in it.

He was staying in Pittsburgh and sticking with the diner. He wasn't bailing. Period.

And his mom? Come hell or high water, she'd go on that round-the-world trip of a lifetime. He hoped it wouldn't be a battle now that he'd be solo, but if it was, he'd find a way to convince Rita to go. Hire somebody. Beg, bribe, or *something*.

Benny had the early shift at The Wanderlust, so Jake didn't need to go in until about eleven. He thought about calling his brothers for a game of pickup basketball, but they'd know immediately something was wrong, and he didn't want to explain or pretend. Besides, he was so ticked that he might get unnecessarily physical.

Rain threatened, but he changed into gym shorts and a t-shirt and grabbed his windbreaker anyway. He drove too fast over to Schenley Park, hoping a long run might help.

He ran too fast. Pushing himself. Trying to expel the feeling of betrayal that burnt him so badly. Taking his stupid choices out on his body.

What an idiot he'd been to think that just because he'd fallen in love—head over foolish heels—that Sadie had, too. What a dolt he was that he hadn't said anything. It would have killed him to find out she didn't feel the same, but at least he'd have known sooner. He could have chosen to enter a farce of a marriage to keep up the charade for his mom. Or maybe self-preservation would have saved him.

Finally, Jake came to a stop and bent over, hands on knees, as he gasped for air. It wasn't just the hard run. He was spent, mentally and emotionally.

When he stood, he spotted a bench and made his way

over to it. He collapsed there, ignoring its wet surface. He sat and stared at nothing, letting grass and trees and people blur into something he barely saw, until a young couple crossed the path directly in front of him. Pressed tightly together, the man held an oversized umbrella over them both and said something to the woman. She laughed, rosy-cheeked and very pregnant. In love. Obviously.

Jake looked away, chilled by cooling sweat, a damp seat, and bone-deep disappointment.

He shoved his hands in his pockets. Something poked his finger, and he pulled out the Pirates ticket from the game he'd attended with Sadie. The one where she'd said yes to his grand plan. He'd kept it on purpose, thinking someday it'd be a helluva memento.

Why? Because he'd been so hopeful—sitting at PNC Park with a woman whose kiss he couldn't forget and a future of shiny possibility stretching out before him. Because that visit to True Springs was so fresh in his mind. The hotel manager who'd claimed that the natural spring water had some sort of magical quality, that the establishment owners spiked everything they made with it, that he might just find true love…

Jake had scoffed at the time. He'd only been looking for a change, not for love. But through a twist of fate and a big idea, he'd rediscovered Sadie. Love had found him, or so he'd thought.

He couldn't have been more wrong.

Jake tore the ticket in half, in half again, and then in as many pieces as the stiff paper would allow. Then he hauled himself up and shoved it unceremoniously into the nearest trash can.

He'd have to do the same to his marriage. Get it annulled.

It wasn't real anyway. Not to Sadie.

22

Sadie slept late the next morning as a result of tossing and turning half the night. But when she woke, she knew. Just as Rita said, Sadie knew that what she'd envisioned was both what she truly wanted *and* the best choice —because it *felt* right.

The question now was what to do about it.

She winced. No, the real question was: could Jake forgive her?

Sadie wasn't scheduled at the diner this morning, but she knew Jake was. It didn't matter that she had hours before his shift ended; she felt a strong urge to hurry.

She popped a shower cap over her head, peeled off her pajamas, and hustled into the shower. She worked some magic on her slept-on hair with her favorite Mixed Chicks product, brushed on mascara, and dressed in the skirt and pink t-shirt Jake had liked so much—this time with a bra. She made herself eat a granola bar and drink a glass of milk for fortification, then pedaled over to The Wanderlust.

She thought hard the whole way about what she'd say and how best to approach him. It could be busy, and she didn't want to cause a big scene. On the other hand, she didn't want to wait until he got off shift. She didn't want to wait another minute.

After locking up her bike, Sadie slipped in the back door and snatched her apron off the hook. She ducked back out and went around to the front entrance.

Rita was hostessing, and raised her eyebrows when she saw Sadie.

Sadie smiled tremulously and put a finger to her lips. "I have a plan. Sit me like a customer, out of view of the kitchen. Tell Denise not to mention me to Jake, okay?"

Rita inclined her head, led her to table eighteen (a booth by the front window as far from the kitchen as you could get), and handed her a menu. Then she reached out and squeezed Sadie's hand. Rita knew what her being here meant.

Sadie was making a play for Jake. For keeps. She was staying.

If he'd have her.

Jake was busy dumping veggies on an omelet, chocolate chips in a pancake, and burning some bacon for a Black and Gold. Nearly lunchtime, but everyone still wanted breakfast. It didn't matter to him. He was just trying hard not to think, grilling and frying like an automaton.

Rita clipped a ticket up and slid it over. She walked away, and he reached for it.

As soon as his fingers touched the paper, he got a shock and snatched his fingers back.

No—not a shock, more like a zing. From paper. He shook his head at the oddity. Man, he thought, he really was off today.

He peered at the ticket, ready to throw together whatever was needed. But the words weren't the usual diner lingo and abbreviations he expected. Jake slid both the omelet and the pancake to waiting plates, then pulled the strange ticket from the clip to look more closely.

It wasn't Rita's writing…

It was Sadie's.

He sucked in a deep breath—hope rising so swiftly that his head nearly swam—and read:

RUSH ORDER:
   1 *REAL* marriage, hold the travel
   1 perfect husband, with a side of Diner Boy
   1 honeymoon to True Springs—or chef's choice
   Unlimited helping of true love

Jake's skin tingled and his blood rushed. His heart felt like it could soar.

Sadie was here. And Sadie wanted to stay. She was asking to marry him—to stay married to him—for real. And he needed to give her an answer.

He was nearly at the door and then remembered the bacon. He dashed back to the grill and shoved it onto a plate. That order could wait. This one couldn't.

Jake yanked off his apron and, order ticket in hand,

bolted from the kitchen. As soon as he came through the doors, he found Sadie seated at a far table, her hands clasped and her posture tense.

He strode from behind the counter directly to her. She stood and met him halfway. They didn't break eye contact.

"I'm not going abroad. It's only you I want. I love you. I don't want to be anywhere you aren't," Sadie said, rushing as if she needed to get the worlds out first thing. She took a deep breath. "If you'll still have me?"

"I will." Jake grinned because it reminded him of their wedding day. "I love you too."

"Thank God," she said, and dove into his chest. Jake wrapped his arms around her, dropped his head to hers, and closed his eyes as he breathed her in.

She pulled back enough to look up at him. "I'm so sorry," she whispered. "I should have told you right off."

"Me too." Jake took her face in his hands and kissed her. "I should have told you I loved you way back when I realized it."

She rose on tiptoes and kissed him again—a hard press that told him she would never tire of hearing those three words.

"Let's start over," he said.

"For real this time," Sadie said, and her face glowed with happiness.

"For real," Jake said with the same joy blazing in his chest.

Ticket still in hand, Jake picked her up and spun Sadie around. Neither even registered the clapping.

———

Thank you for reading *Faking It Together* and the *Love That Lasts* series! Ready for Jeremy's story? He thinks he's immune to the magic of love and he knows for sure he can't trust Darcy. She didn't just walk away from him last time, she ran…

Darcy desperately needs a new beginning, a do-over, a fresh start. And she can have it all—if only she can land Jeremy's popular neighborhood music club as her first client and score a second chance with him.

Jeremy needs to suck it up, sell his soul, and accept her big bucks to save his club. Except he doesn't want Darcy in his life—not in his business, his head, or even his bed.

Is the forced proximity of working together too great a risk to their battered hearts—or worth the chance to rekindle their past love?

Turn the page for a sneak peek at *Second Chance Love Affair*!

SECOND CHANCE LOVE AFFAIR

Chapter 1

Jeremy Walker had never felt his body strain viscerally in two different directions, until Darcy Hellston walked through his music club's door in the middle of the day with a briefcase. Opposing instincts warred. Stay, speak, beg—because *dammit*, he still wanted her. Avoid, hide, run—because Darcy was the only woman that held the power to crush him.

"Hi," she said. Darcy stepped forward, then back, then extended a hand halfway, then dropped it awkwardly.

Yeah, Jeremy thought, a real dilemma. You didn't shake with someone you'd shared mind-blowing sex with, and you sure as hell didn't hug someone you'd blown off. He stood stock-still.

She regrouped. "I'm glad to catch you here."

"What do you want?" He refused to play games with her.

Last he'd seen her, her light blond hair had been down

and mussed from his hands. Now it was pulled back tight. Much like the look in her hazel eyes, it shouted no nonsense. She sucked in a breath, her chest filling, shoulders shifting back. "I have a proposal for you. For Vine, that is."

Business? Really? He couldn't help a twitch of the eyebrow, which she must have taken as interest.

"I'd like to invest."

There went those diametrically opposed cells again. He was lucky his head didn't blow right off his shoulders.

And how the hell did she know that he needed a cash infusion for Vine? He'd put out feelers, he'd talked to a few people with connections—

Ah, their mutual friend Peter's wedding festivities. Someone must have told her. That sucked. He rubbed a hand over his face. He'd have preferred that the financial health of his venture remain private.

Darcy didn't wait for him to speak, just turned to the bar, pulled out a stool, and, despite the formfitting skirt and heels, hopped right up. Next thing he knew, she'd flipped open a leather folio that held an electronic tablet and propped it up. A swipe of her finger across the screen, and the words Hellston Enterprises showed up on a blue background.

She glanced over her shoulder. "Please sit." She pointed to the stool next to her.

"I've got a lot to do before opening," he said.

"I promise I won't take more than a few minutes of your time." She swiped again, and a large sum—more even than he needed—caught his eye at the bottom of a simple spreadsheet.

He chose the next stool over, leaving one in between—

a barricade to touching her. He crossed his arms over his chest and clenched his jaw.

"It's not unusual that small businesses incur more costs than expected during startup," she began, sliding the tablet closer to him. She spelled out her plan to buoy Vine's bottom line, and the numbers were sound. Actually, her terms were more than generous. Far more generous than the other offer he had on the table. And she hadn't been kidding; she was done with her pitch in no time. So fast, in fact, that he'd barely had time to think it through. It was straightforward, and he couldn't point out any holes in her logic or anything that should give him pause.

Only his instincts had serious misgivings about accepting Darcy's offer to invest in Vine. The club was *his*. And she was... Well, they had history. A history that was the polar opposite of the buttoned-up, briefcase-toting, all-business version of her that balanced precariously on his barstool in a pencil skirt and heels right now. Even her bare legs—reasonable, given that it was late August—which he'd been trying to keep his eyes off, didn't offset the prim appearance.

On the other hand, Vine needed this kind of cash infusion. The one offer he had was from a small startup group —in other words, a trio of pals that were looking to get in on the ground floor of something big. They didn't hold a candle to Hellston confidence-wise. Despite the fact that Vine was starting to gain traction in the Pittsburgh music scene, it was still very small potatoes as far as investors were concerned. He doubted he'd have a third offer. And he'd never have Hellston's interest if it wasn't for the personal connection with Darcy.

Darcy clasped her hands in her lap, yet she flipped the

stylus over and over in her fingers. Her foot ticked up and down in an impatient rhythm. If her jitters were any indication, she was nervous. Did she have something at stake here, too? More than just a business deal?

Though he sat, his feet were planted firmly and he widened his stance. "What's in it for you?"

"The interest, of course," she said, looking at him like he'd missed the point.

"What else?"

"Helping small businesses can be really rewarding." She glanced away, then back. "I told you. You've got a good thing going. I believe if we build you a longer runway, you can really take off."

She wasn't telling him quite everything, he thought. But he also didn't sense that her reticence was anything sinister or sneaky. Maybe her business role simply required tight lips. Was he willing to take this money, to owe more money, to keep his dream alive, even without full disclosure from her?

She fumbled the stylus, recovered it, set it down next to her portfolio, then angled her shoulders toward him again.

Darcy opened her mouth at the same time he did, but he spoke first. "I have another offer. Why should I choose Hellston?"

For a second she froze, then her shoulders and hands both opened up. "Well, it's *Hellston*."

He rose from the stool and moved a few feet away. He put his hands on his hips and stared without seeing much.

"I'm happy to answer more questions," she said.

Jeremy remembered all the way back to their time together at Glenmead College when those same lips stretched in a wide, uninhibited laugh. She'd had a surprisingly good singing voice and often belted out lyrics without getting a single word wrong. The kind of girl who just had to dance if there was a band. Band or event t-shirts, cut-off shorts that highlighted her long, lean legs, flip-flops and a toe ring. And later, naked limbs and an enthusiastic, vocal lover who he'd find still burrowed into him when he woke. A friend and lover who was nearly always at his side—before she'd flaked out and disappeared on him, that was.

When he'd seen her at the wedding of one of their college roommates in True Springs a few months ago, it'd been awkward at first. He hadn't been nursing a grudge, but she'd showed her true colors when she vanished, and that had shifted things for him. Plus, she seemed so different from the young woman he remembered—all banker's wife or some shit, despite having no ring on her finger. She wore flattering, classy clothing, tame but clearly expensive jewelry, and a reserved demeanor he couldn't reconcile.

However, between the rehearsal dinner, the wedding, the celebratory vibe, and the free-flowing alcohol, she'd loosened up. So had he. They'd gravitated toward each other like they always had. Things had gotten hot. They'd spent a stunner of a night together—and then she'd crushed him. Again.

Only a few weeks ago, she'd shown up at one of Vine's pricier events. Of course he'd given her the event ticket in True Springs, but he was shocked as hell she'd used it. After all, she'd made it clear she hadn't wanted to continue to see him. And that night at Vine? She'd stuck to that—hadn't even searched him out to say hello.

Except here she was again. In his club. Searching him out. Somehow—miraculously, uncannily, suspiciously— offering him exactly what he needed. Financially, anyway.

"So, what do you say?" she asked.

He turned back to her and saw she wore a polite smile. Her knees were pressed together, her ankles were crossed daintily, her hands sat clasped in her lap, and her back was straight.

Her demure, classy appearance didn't matter. If he took her up on this offer, it'd be like making a deal with the devil. It had taken him years to get over her after college, but that chance encounter in True Springs brought it home. She had been under his skin all that time, and having a taste of her made him want her in a big way all over again. He wished he could just flip a switch and turn it off, like killing the music from the club's sound system, but it wasn't that easy. Which sucked.

"I'll get back to you," he said.

Her shoulders dropped a fraction of an inch and a bit of light went out of her eyes. "You used to be the most decisive person I'd ever met."

This was a big flipping deal, as far as he was concerned. Big enough he wanted to roll it around awhile. He shrugged. "I'm not sure I want to be indebted to a woman who thinks George Michael is the be-all end-all."

Just like that, her eyes shone bright again, and a happy smile erupted. He felt a little like he'd gotten the wind knocked out of him. What had possessed him to reference that old, silly argument?

"So," she said, "should I—"

Jeremy spun and headed for the back. "I've got work to do."

She could forget the pushy sales tactics. He'd said he'd let her know, and he would. In his own time. In the meanwhile, she had found the door on the way in; she could surely find it on the way out.

———

I hope you enjoyed this sneak peek and will read *Second Chance Love Affair* next!

———

Love That Lasts series:

Faking It Together (#1)
Second Chance Love Affair (#2)
Dreaming of Forever with You (#3)
Starting Over Together (#4)
and
Making Forever with You (Prequel
—co-authored with Savannah Kade!)

THANKS AND MORE

I'm so thrilled you found *Faking It Together*! Would you kindly share your enjoyment of the story by leaving a brief review on Goodreads, BookBub, or your retailer? Reviews and word of mouth (*please do tell a friend!*) are still the best way for readers to find books they'll love. So grateful for each and every review—thank you!

I love to hear from readers, and these days there are so many ways for us to connect! On my website (www. jbschroederauthor.com), you can subscribe to my newsletter to have news delivered right to your email inbox or visit the Finding JB page to reach me via my social media links—choose what works for you. If you prefer *only* new release alerts, however, simply follow me on BookBub or Amazon.

ACKNOWLEDGMENTS

I couldn't have launched a single book without my tribe: fellow authors, willing readers, and incredibly supportive friends and family. So, bear with me, and please excuse my many exclamation marks:

Essential to *Love that Lasts* series:

Kate Schroeder: My heart, my pride, my partner in crime from the initial seed of an idea. It wouldn't have been half as much fun without you. *Still* laughing over alphabet brainstorming!

Savannah Kade and Eli Collier: for your immediate enthusiasm, unconditional support, indie smarts, and always—your friendship. I'd be lost without you!

Jessica Orbock: for your thoughts on the legal side of things. Always helpful to have expert advice!

Stacey Wilk: writing friends are the best at impromptu brainstorming. Thank you for the major light bulb moment!

Key for the *Faking It Together* story:

Kelsey Scout, Nora Baron, Richard Henry Schaefer III, and Deb Lindh: intrepid souls who've taught abroad and thoroughly answered my shout out for help!

Tammy King and Deb Garlock: thank you for being my go-to 'burgh ladies!

Jennifer Richter: my gratitude for supporting a local author. Hope your daughters get a kick out of seeing their names in print—when they are old enough!

Johanna Ojeda: little did you know I was listening with an ulterior motive! Thank you for the clarity on dealing with challenging hair.

Aquila Editing, Editing720, and Jen Coleman: you make up a stellar team!

All the Pittsburgh folks: *you* make Pittsburgh special. There's no place like home!

Overall:

Despite all the help, I take sole credit for any mistakes.

And last but never least, dear reader: my heartfelt thanks for reading and reviewing!

ABOUT THE AUTHOR

JB SCHROEDER, a graduate of Penn State University's creative writing program, writes both contemporary romance and romantic suspense—in other words: *romance to make your heart race*. She adores stories about everyday people embracing new beginnings—especially when the characters need a little help from true love.

www.jbschroederauthor.com

9 781943 561193